Angel

Annabelle Starr

EGMONT

Special thanks to:

Kirsty Neale, St John's Walworth Church of England
School and Belmont Primary School

EGMONT

We bring stories to life

Published in Great Britain 2007
by Egmont UK Limited
239 Kensington High Street, London W8 6SA

Text & illustrations © 2007 Egmont UK Ltd
Text by Kirsty Neale
Illustrations by Helen Turner

The moral rights of the author and illustrator have been asserted

ISBN 978 1 4052 3245 6

1 3 5 7 9 10 8 6 4 2

A CIP catalogue record for this title is available
from the British Library

Typeset by Avon DataSet Ltd, Bidford on Avon, Warwickshire
Printed and bound in Great Britain by the CPI Group

'I like a bit of a mystery, so I thought it was very good'
Phoebe, age 10

'I liked the way there's stuff about modelling and make-up, cos that's what girls like'
Beth M, age 11

'Great idea – very cool! Not for boys . . .'
Louise, age 9

'I really enjoyed reading the books. They keep you on your toes and the characters are really interesting (I love the illustrations!) . . . They balance out humour and suspense'
Beth R, age 10

'Exciting and quite unpredictable. I like that the girls do the detective work'
Lauren, age 10

'All the characters are very realistic. I would definitely recommend these to a friend'
Krystyna, age 9

We want to know what *you* think about *Megastar Mysteries*! Visit:

www.mega-star.co.uk

for loads of coolissimo megastar stuff to do!

Meet the
Megastar Mysteries Team!

Hi, this is me, **Rosie Parker** (otherwise known as Nosy Parker), and these are my best mates . . .

. . . **Soph** (Sophie) **McCoy** – she's a real fashionista sista – and . . .

. . . **Abs** (Abigail) **Flynn**, who's officially une grande genius.

Here's my mum, **Liz Parker**. Much to my embarrassment, her fashion and music taste is well and truly stuck in the 1980s (but despite all that I still love her dearly) . . .

. . . and my nan, **Pam Parker**, the murder-mystery freak I mentioned on the cover. Sometimes, just sometimes, her crackpot ideas do come in handy.

Consider yourself introduced!

ROSIE'S MINI MEGASTAR PHRASEBOOK

Want to speak our lingo, but don't know your soeurs from your signorinas? No problemo! Just use my comprehensive guide . . .

-a-rama	add this ending to a word to indicate a large quantity: e.g. 'The after-show party was celeb-a-rama'
amigo	Spanish for 'friend'
au contraire, mon frère	French for 'on the contrary, my brother'
au revoir	French for 'goodbye'
barf/barfy/barfissimo	sick/sick-making/very sick-making indeed
bien sûr, ma soeur	French for 'of course, my sister'
bon	French for 'good'
bonjour	French for 'hello'
celeb	short for 'celebrity'
convo	short for 'conversation'
cringe-fest	a highly embarrassing situation
Cringeville	a place we all visit from time to time when something truly embarrassing happens to us
cringeworthy	an embarrassing person, place or thing might be described as this
daggy	Australian for 'unfashionable' or unstylish'
doco	short for 'documentary'
exactamundo	not a real foreign word, but a great way to express your agreement with someone
exactement	French for 'exactly'

excusez moi	French for 'excuse me'
fashionista	'a keen follower of fashion' – can be teamed with 'sista' for added rhyming fun
glam	short for 'glamorous'
gorge/gorgey	short for 'gorgeous': e.g. 'the lead singer of that band is gorge/gorgey'
hilarioso	not a foreign word at all, just a great way to liven up 'hilarious'
hola, señora	Spanish for 'hello, missus'
hottie	no, this is *not* short for hot water bottle – it's how you might describe an attractive-looking boy to your friends
-issimo	try adding this ending to English adjectives for extra emphasis: e.g. coolissimo, crazissimo – très funissimo, non?
je ne sais pas	French for 'I don't know'
je voudrais un beau garçon, s'il vous plaît	French for 'I would like an attractive boy, please'
journos	short for 'journalists'
les Français	French for, erm, 'the French'
Loserville	this is where losers live, particularly evil school bully Amanda Hawkins
mais	French for 'but'
marvelloso	not technically a foreign word, just a more exotic version of 'marvellous'
massivo	Italian for 'massive'
mon amie/mes amis	French for 'my friend'/'my friends'
muchos	Spanish for 'many'

non	French for 'no'
nous avons deux garçons ici	French for 'we have two boys here'
no way, José!	'that's never going to happen!'
oui	French for 'yes'
quelle horreur!	French for 'what horror!'
quelle surprise!	French for 'what a surprise!'
sacré bleu	French for 'gosh' or even 'blimey'
stupido	this is the Italian for 'stupid' – stupid!
-tastic	add this ending to any word to indicate a lot of something: e.g. 'Abs is braintastic'
très	French for 'very'
swoonsome	decidedly attractive
si, si, signor/signorina	Italian for 'yes, yes, mister/miss'
terriblement	French for 'terribly'
une grande	French for 'a big' – add the word 'genius' and you have the perfect description of Abs
Vogue	it's only the world's most influential fashion magazine, darling!
voilà	French for 'there it is'
what's the story, Rory?	'what's going on?'
what's the plan, Stan?	'which course of action do you think we should take?'
what the crusty old grandads?	'what on earth?'
zut alors!	French for 'darn it!'

Hi Megastar reader!

My name's Annabelle Starr*. I'm a fashion stylist – just like Soph's Aunt Penny – which means it's my job to help celebrities look their best at all times.

Over the years, I've worked with all sorts of big names, some of whom also have seriously big egos! Take the time I flew all the way to Japan to style a shoot for a girl band. One of the members refused to wear the designer number I'd picked out for her and insisted on sporting a dress her mum had run up from some revolting old curtains instead. The only way I could get her to take it off was to persuade her it didn't match her pet Pekinese's outfit!

Anyway, when I first started out, I never dreamt I'd write a series of books based around my crazy celebrity experiences, but that's just what I've done with Megastar Mysteries. Rosie, Soph and Abs have just the sort of adventures I wish my friends and I could have got up to when we were teenagers!

I really hope you enjoy reading the books as much as I enjoyed writing them!

Love **Annabelle**

* I'll let you in to a little secret: this isn't my real name, but in this business you can never be too careful!

Chapter One

Wednesday lunchtimes totally rock.

OK, so I don't usually spend them in the most glamorous location. The third table across from the tray-stack in our grotty school canteen is about as un-glamorous as it gets. But Wednesday is the day my all-time fave celeb gossip mag, *Star Secrets*, comes out each week. Why so marvelloso, I hear you ask?

Top ten cool things about *Star Secrets*:

1. Well, duh – it's full of celeb gossip. I'm not

called Nosy Parker cos I've got a big nose.

2. It's got photos of celebs doing dead ordinary stuff, like emptying the bin in their bunny slippers and no make-up.

3. They have a TV guide that has not been drawn all over in blue biro by my nan, who is obsessed with remembering when her favourite murder-mystery shows are on.

4. The 'Dating or Ditching?' section tells you which stars are going out with each other, so you know which boy-celebs are available and worth fancying.

5. Last week, their astrologer, Destiny Blake, predicted I'd find myself in a sticky situation with a friend. The next day, I sat on a lump of chewing gum on the bus and it went all over the jeans I was wearing, which belonged to Abs. Spooky, eh?

6. They gave the first single by Fusion (lead singer Maff, très gorge singer and co-snogger for my first snog) five stars out of five, which means they have genius taste in music.

7. The fashion pages, titled 'Fashion Passion', are written by it-girl and top style guru, Roma Richie. She's ace. Even Soph agrees with me on that.

8. It's about PROPER music – NOT the eighties kind I am forced to listen to at home by Mum.

9. Dreamy boy posters – not only good for delish-ness, but also for covering up the disgusting flowery wallpaper I am not allowed to redecorate in my bedroom.

10. They have interviews with stars full of info on celeb-ness that could be very handy when I am a rich and famous writer.

'So, what's new?' said Abs, as I flicked through the glossy pages one particularly gossip-worthy Wednesday lunchtime.

She was sitting opposite me at our usual table, along with my other best mate, Soph, who I knew was itching to get her hands on the mag for the fashion pages.

'Mirage Mullins' new haircut,' I announced. 'Do we like?'

Abs and Soph leaned over to study *Star Secrets*'s double-page photo spread of Mirage and her freshly styled choppy bob. Ever since we helped Mirage Mullins out a few months ago, we've sort of felt connected to her, even if she is a mega-successful celeb and we're just three ordinary-ish schoolgirls.

'We like *a lot*,' said Soph. She pulled a strand of her own brown, wavy hair forwards and studied it intently. 'D'you think mine would look good like that?'

'Er, Soph,' said Abs, who was busy investigating the contents of her packed lunch. (Her dad makes these totally random sandwich combos and by the look on Abs's face, today's filling – beetroot, cheese spread and tuna – wasn't going down as an all-time classic.) 'You had to nag your mum for, like, a year before she let you buy hair-straighteners. I don't think she'll be saying yes to blonde highlights and spiky bits any time soon.'

'Hmm,' Soph frowned. She flipped over a few pages of the magazine, still leaning across the table and twirling her hair. 'I do quite fancy a change, though.'

'Look!' I said, suddenly spotting another familiar face as the pages fell open at 'Fashion Passion'. 'It's Angel.'

Soph grabbed the magazine and pulled it across the table to get a better look.

'Model of the moment, Angel, works the red carpet in one of this season's hottest designer trends,' she read aloud from the caption under Angel's photo.

'She looks gorgeous,' said Abs, peering over her shoulder.

'Totally,' I agreed.

'That dress is seriously coolissimo,' breathed Soph.

Angel is a HUGE star. Her real name's Jenny Gabriel and, amazing as it sounds, she was a pupil here at Whitney High until she won a modelling contest last year. Soph is one of her biggest fans.

As she likes to point out whenever anyone mentions Angel (and quite often when they don't), she's proof that fashion dreams really can come true. Angel's younger sister, Francesca, is in Abs's class, so we sometimes get to hear what she's up to. Frankie's almost as gorgeous as Angel herself, but for some très bonkers reason she doesn't fancy a life of glamour, showbiz parties and earning piles of cash for pouting her way down a catwalk. She's planning to be a famous artist instead. I honestly have no idea why anyone would want to spend all day getting paint under their fingernails and then having to cut off their ear or drown half a cow, or any of that weird stuff artists do to get famous. I did quite like the one who didn't make her bed for a whole year and called it art, although there'd be fat chance of getting away with that in *my* house.

'Earth to Rosie. Rosie, this is Earth calling,' I suddenly heard Abs say.

'What?' I said, snapping out of my mini-daydream.

'Duh!' said Soph, pointing down at the mag. It

was now lying open on a page that featured a massivo close-up of Angel's face – the kind of pic that's guaranteed to show up even the tiniest lurking spot and, in my case, that pokey bit of eyebrow that won't lie flat whatever I do to it. 'The new Teen Shimmer colours,' said Soph, still pointing at Angel's face. It was an advert. In one corner of the page, just by Angel's perfectly pointy chin, were the words:

Angel: The Face of Teen Shimmer

Angel wears Emerald City Eye Shine, LushLash Mascara in Chocolate Brown, Cheeky Pink Blush and Pucker Up Glimmer-Gloss, all from the brand new range of Teen Shimmer colours. COMING SOON to a beauty counter near you!

'Just imagine,' said Soph, dreamily, 'being the face of Teen Shimmer. All that free make-up. Every single shade of lippy. Enough nail varnish to paint every one of your fingernails and toenails a different colour . . .'

'Why would you do that?' asked Abs.

'I wouldn't,' said Soph. 'Probably. It's just you'd have enough nail varnish if you wanted to do it.'

'Just think,' I said, 'this time last year, Angel was stuck here, eating lunch in this very canteen, with nothing to look forward to except double science on a Wednesday afternoon. And now look at her.'

'It's like a fairytale,' sighed Soph.

Me and Abs smirked.

'It *is*,' Soph protested. 'She was in this totally cool *Vogue* fashion shoot last month, and she's always doing the big catwalk shows. And we all saw that billboard opposite the bus stop. It was enormous. Her head was about the same size as the bus.'

'A bit like Amanda Hawkins's head, come to think of it,' I said, spotting my least favourite person in the entire world walking across the canteen towards us.

'What's up with you lot?' she snapped, as the three of us collapsed in a fit of giggles.

'Nothing you'd be interested in,' I said.

She threw a haughty glance at the magazine, which was still lying open on the table. 'Jenny Gabriel?' she scoffed. 'You're right – I'm not interested, and I don't know why anyone else is either.'

'Jealous much?' hissed Soph under her breath as Amanda stalked off.

'Course she is,' I said. 'She can't *stand* anyone who gets more attention than her.'

Abs nodded wisely. 'There's your fairytale, Soph,' she said. 'Starring Amanda Hawkins as the wicked witch.'

* * *

By the time I got home that afternoon, I was exhausted. Mum's always moaning about how hard she works at the council offices and OK, she does get home quite a bit later than I do, but at least she doesn't have to sit through French, maths *and* double science on a Wednesday afternoon. Or, for that matter, do homework. Don't teachers realise we have better things to do? Important stuff, like watching *EastEnders* or trying to decide whether Justin Timberlake is cuter than Orlando Bloom. Luckily, just as I was about to start Madame Bertillon's mountain of French homework, Soph's instant-messaging username flashed up on my computer, quickly followed by Abs's, and saved me from death-by-boredom:

FashionPolice: Have you seen latest on the *Star Secrets* website?
CutiePie: Non.
NosyParker: SPILL!
FashionPolice: Très bad. They're saying Angel looks v. thin and is acting weird.
NosyParker: You lie.
FashionPolice: Au contraire, mon doubting frère. Only a rumour, but says she got sent home from a photoshoot last week for acting stroppy.
CutiePie: That so doesn't sound like her.
NosyParker: She was always a real laugh at school.

CutiePie: No way fame would change her that much.

FashionPolice: Or make her lose loads of weight. Stick-thin models are sooo last year.

NosyParker: Has Frankie said anything?

CutiePie: Nope.

FashionPolice: Maybe not true, then.

CutiePie: Rumours suck!

NosyParker: So does French homework.

FashionPolice: Oui, oui, mon amie.

It was pretty weird. I read *Star Secrets* all the time and they're nearly always right, but I totally couldn't imagine Angel throwing a showbiz strop. She was in the year above me, Soph and Abs, but she was always really friendly. We went to Frankie's birthday party one year and Angel was a right laugh. We played loads of really stupid party games, like Sardines and Twister and Murder in the Dark and even though she was older than most people at the party, she joined in with everything and wasn't stuck up at all.

Soph was right, though – it *was* only a rumour. I looked at the stack of French homework sitting on my desk, and tried to put Angel and *Star Secrets* right out of my mind.

As les Français would say, it was très difficile, considering.

Chapter Two

The next week was boring but busy. Before I knew it, Wednesday had come round again and I was dashing into the newsagent's on my way to school.

'Morning, Rosie,' said Mrs Campbell from behind the counter. She's a friend of Nan's and keeps trying to persuade me to buy magazines that she thinks are 'improving' instead of just gossipy. I mean, as if that's ever going to happen.

'Hi, Mrs C,' I said, heading for the magazine racks.

Three, two, one . . .

'There's a lovely new issue of *Nice Knits* just come in,' she said.

Bingo.

I scanned the shelves for *Star Secrets'* familiar purple logo and celeb-sprinkled cover, pretending I hadn't heard.

'*Nice Knits.* It's down there on the left,' Mrs Campbell persisted.

I stopped dead in my tracks.

'That's right, dear,' she said, happily. 'Just by your knee, under *Barn Owl Monthly.* Which is another smashing one, if you're looking for something a bit more outdoorsy.'

But, surprisingly, it wasn't *Nice Knits,* or even *Barn Owl Monthly* I was looking at. It was *Star Secrets* and, splashed right across the front, under a headline that screamed 'IS IT ALL OVER FOR ANGEL?' was a picture of Jenny Gabriel. She looked pale, thin and not much like her normal gorgeous self.

I picked up a copy and handed it to Mrs Campbell. 'Just this, thanks,' I said, still frowning at the picture.

'Oh. Well, if you're sure.' She sounded disappointed, although why I don't know. I've been buying the same magazine every Wednesday for the last two years. And every Wednesday she tries to change my mind and fails, so you'd really think she would be used to it by now. That's grey-haired old ladies for you, though. If they're not dangerously obsessed with biscuits and murder-mystery shows, they're trying to improve your brain.

'Bye, Rosie dear,' Mrs Campbell called after me as I left.

I opened the magazine and found the Angel article. It was right at the front and pretty long. On one side of the page there was a blurry close-up of Angel looking even worse than she did on the cover. The other side had a Roma Richie exclusive. No way could this wait until I got to school. Besides, the last time I tried reading a magazine in registration, Mr Adams (form teacher and swoonsome lurve-god) confiscated it. Soph reckons she saw him reading it through the staffroom door at lunchtime, while we were starved of our weekly celeb-fest.

I folded the magazine in half so it didn't flop about, checked the pavement ahead for big holes and dog poo, then started to walk, reading as I went.

ANGEL'S CAREER IN CRISIS

Roma Richie reports

Top model Angel was last week sent home from a photoshoot after dramatically fainting in front of the cameras. *Star Secrets* can exclusively reveal it wasn't the first time this has happened. Jenny 'Angel' Gabriel shot to fame last year after winning a contract with leading modelling agency, SuperModels. Her angelic looks and positive attitude quickly made her a favourite with many designers. But according to a fashion-industry insider, Angel has become difficult and unreliable, passing out at three photoshoots in the last month. 'She's lost loads of weight,' the insider told your *Star Secrets* reporter. 'Plenty of models are thin, but Angel is really skinny and it looks unhealthy.

She seems tired all the time and at least one magazine had to airbrush her photos because her skin is so bad.'

Sadly, many models suffer from being over-worked. Is Angel just another victim?

When we asked her agency, a spokesperson denied Angel was being overworked. 'We keep a very close eye on the hours all our models work,' the spokesperson claimed, adding that Angel has simply been feeling under the weather for the past few weeks. Whatever the truth behind these rumours, there's no doubt Angel's halo is in serious danger of slipping.

'Hola, señora,' said Soph, coming up behind me just as I finished reading.

'Have you seen this?' I said. I was in shock.

Soph grabbed the magazine as soon as she clapped eyes on Angel's photo, and read the article. She's much faster at reading gossip than she is when we have to share a book in English.

'Zut alors!' said Soph, folding up the mag and handing it back to me. 'I can't believe it.'

'I know.'

'She must just be ill,' Soph reasoned. 'Like the bit at the bottom says. "Under the weather".'

'I s'pose.'

The truth was, I didn't really know what to think. I mean, first of all, 'under the weather'. What the crusty old grandads does that mean? We're all under the weather. If we weren't, we wouldn't get a suntan on the two days every year when it's sunny, and we wouldn't get wet the rest of the time when it rains. I also wouldn't arrive at school on windy days looking like I have a bird's nest for hair. If Angel was ill, why didn't her spokesperson just say that? And did just being ill make you lose that much weight? The bit about Angel being 'difficult and unreliable' was even harder to imagine, but why would *Star Secrets* print something if it wasn't true? My fave magazine or my fave model – it was très, très tricky to know who to believe.

At break, me, Abs and Soph found a quiet corner and settled down for a good goss about what was going on. Unfortunately, Amanda

Hawkins and her cronies also decided it was an ideal spot to start planning their latest evil scheme, and plonked themselves down nearby. For once, though, they seemed far too interested in themselves to be bothered with making our lives a misery.

'I don't understand,' said Soph. 'If Angel's mega-famous and getting loads of modelling jobs, why would she suddenly start acting like this?'

'And why would she want to get thinner when all those designers loved the way she looked?' Abs added.

'It doesn't look good for Teen Shimmer, either,' I said. 'I mean, Angel's the face of their whole make-up range.'

'Hey,' said Abs, nudging me and pointing. 'It's Frankie.'

Soph bit her lip. 'She must be *sooo* upset by all of this.'

'Yeah, well, I don't think it's about to get any better,' I said. Amanda Hawkins seemed to have spotted Frankie too, and she'd just flashed a seriously nasty grin to the little gang of girls standing around her.

'Oi, Gabriel!' she yelled.

'Uh-oh,' whispered Abs.

Frankie looked up to see who had shouted her name, but she didn't stop or answer Amanda.

'Next time you see your string-bean of a sister, why don't you take her a sandwich or twenty?' Amanda shouted.

Her cronies burst out laughing, and it looked like that was the final straw for Frankie. Her face crumpled and she broke into a run, heading for the toilets.

'That's it,' I said, jumping to my feet and grabbing my book bag.

'Leave it,' groaned Soph, who hates confrontation. 'Let's just go and make sure Frankie's OK.'

'In a minute,' I called over my shoulder, striding over to where Amanda and her stupid gang of mates were still sniggering.

'Look, girls,' said Amanda in a loud voice. 'It's Nosy Parker, come to stick her nosy nose in.'

They laughed again. Honestly, those girls need to get out more if Amanda Hawkins is their idea of funny.

'Me stick my nose in?' I spluttered, indignantly. *Oh, the hypocrisy*, I thought. I didn't say it, though, because Amanda Hawkins isn't the brightest of girls and I wasn't planning on hanging around long enough to start explaining four-syllable words to her. 'What about you, sticking your nose into Frankie's private family problems?' I said. 'You couldn't keep your mouth shut, could you?'

'Where's the fun in that?' she sneered.

'D'you know, Amanda,' I said in the snootiest voice I could manage, 'if brains were chocolate, you wouldn't have enough to cover a peanut.'

And before she had a chance to realise what I'd said, I turned round and stalked off, following Abs and Soph towards the toilets.

'Frankie?' called Abs gently when we got inside.

There was no sign of her, but one of the cubicle doors was shut.

'Frankie, it's Abs. I've got Rosie and Soph with

me. We just want to make sure you're OK.'

Slowly, the door opened and Frankie came out, clutching a soggy, crumpled-up tissue. She looked awful. Her face was streaked with tears and her eyes were all puffy. Her normally sleek and shiny blonde hair was straggly and she was much paler than usual.

'It's OK,' I said, as she glanced nervously towards the door. 'It's just us three.'

She sniffed and tried to smile. 'I'm fine, really. Just not in the mood for Amanda.'

'Who would be?' said Abs.

'She's such a witch,' added Soph.

We led Frankie over to the bench under the coat-hooks and all of us sat down.

'Not everyone thinks like Amanda,' I said. 'We all saw the article, but it just doesn't sound like Angel. She was always so sweet.'

Frankie didn't say anything. She just sat there and these two fat tears plopped down her face and on to her school skirt. I felt humongously sorry for her and madder than ever at Amanda Hawkins.

'I'm so scared,' Frankie hiccupped. 'I don't know what's wrong with her. No one does. Mum and Dad are frantic about it all.'

I put my arm round her shoulders and Abs found her a clean tissue.

'Does she –' Soph began, tentatively. 'I mean, y'know, look after herself properly? Modelling's a really hectic business – there can't be much time to rest between appointments for someone as high-profile as Angel.'

Frankie shook her head. 'No way. Jenny's totally sensible about all that, and SuperModels really do take care of her.' She paused for a minute. 'The rest of the stupid article is more or less true, though. She *has* lost a ton of weight and she *does* keep fainting.'

'Has she been to the doctor?' asked Abs.

'Yeah,' said Frankie. 'They told her it was probably stress and she should take a few weeks off, but . . .' She started crying really hard again, and none of us knew what to do.

If Nan was here, she'd have whipped the tea

and biscuits out in a flash. She reckons there's nothing a nice cup of tea can't solve, including most wars. I swear, if she was in charge of the country, we wouldn't have an army, just a bunch of tea-ladies, ready to leap into action at the first sign of international conflict.

Eventually, Frankie calmed down to that hiccupy stage again.

'I'm really sorry,' she said. 'It's just that – well, Angel doesn't exactly have a choice about taking time off.'

She glanced towards the door again to check nobody was listening.

'With all this bad publicity, no one wants her. She hasn't been booked for a single modelling job.'

Soph's eyes widened. 'What about Teen Shimmer? Surely they haven't dropped her?'

'Not yet,' said Frankie. 'I don't know what she'll do if that happens.'

She blew her nose with a parp so loud it made the rest of us jump. Even Frankie managed a watery sort of laugh as we giggled.

'When Angel got the Teen Shimmer contract, we all thought it was going to be the best thing that ever happened to her,' she said. 'They gave her loads of free make-up –'

Soph threw me and Abs one of her famous I-told-you-so looks.

'– and they were brilliant to work for. Me and Mum and Dad got to go to this big party when they unveiled the first ad and everyone kept saying how amazing Angel was and how perfect she was for Teen Shimmer.'

'That's good,' said Abs. 'They obviously like her, so she's still got at least one job.'

'But that was ages ago,' said Frankie, sounding desperate. 'Everything's changed since then. It's all gone wrong.'

'Is there anything we can do to help?' I said. Honestly, it just kind of slipped out.

Frankie looked surprised. So did Abs and Soph.

'Like what?' said Frankie.

I thought for a minute. I can sniff trouble like my mum can sniff out eighties compilation CDs.

I didn't quite know how, but it seemed as if someone needed to get to the bottom of what was going on with Angel. Someone like me.

'Where's Angel at the moment?' I asked Frankie.

'She's got a really cool flat in London,' said Soph.

We all looked at her.

'What?' she said. 'I read about it in – '

'*Vogue*.' Me and Abs finished the sentence for her.

'Soph's right,' said Frankie. 'She's there at the moment, but she's coming home tomorrow.'

'Aha!' I said, sensing the chance for a bit of detecting.

'SuperModels thought she might get a bit more peace and quiet here, away from the paparazzi,' Frankie explained. 'They've arranged for her to open the new children's wing at the hospital, too. They said it'll be good PR, after all the rumours and the *Star Secrets* article.'

'So when is it?' I asked, feeling half a plan brewing. 'This hospital thingy.'

'Saturday,' said Frankie. 'Do you really think you can help?'

'Do the French eat snails?' I said.

She looked a bit blank.

'Yes, they do,' I assured her.

'She means we'll think of something,' said Abs.

Chapter Three

By Friday afternoon, we still hadn't come up with a better plan than 'go to the hospital and see what happens'. Sheer genius, you have to agree.

'I think we should just pretend to be Angel fans,' Soph said, as we packed our stuff after the end-of-lessons bell. 'Go along as, you know, casual observers.'

'*Pretend* to be Angel fans, Soph?'

'Fine!' she said, in a voice so melodramatic, even Mr Lord (drama teacher and certified no-hoper) would have been impressed. 'We'll go along as *real* fans. But it'll still give us a chance to see what's what.'

'She's right,' said Abs. 'It'll be like the Mirage Mullins situation. We found out loads just by going to see her.'

When we got to the school gates, we agreed to meet at my house the following morning. Abs and Soph headed off, leaving me to climb gracefully into my chauffeur-driven family limo for a smooth, comfortable ride home, with a huge stack of cool CDs to listen to on the awesome in-car sound system.

Oh, no, hang on a minute. I tripped over the step getting on to a dingy double-decker, dragged my book bag up the stairs and fought my way through a bunch of mouthy boys to get a seat, then stuck my MP3 player on as loud as it would go, so I didn't have to listen to them talking about football all the way home. Yes, that's more like it.

As the bus chugged slowly along the high street, I stared out of the window, totally living up to my Nosy Parker nickname. Apart from Lucy Cameron and Ben Taylor from our year at school, snogging outside Top Choonz (I so didn't know they were going out together and I bet no one else does, either), there wasn't much going on. But as we stopped at the traffic lights, I spotted a familiar blonde head. The bus moved forward a few metres, and I pressed my nose right against the glass to get a better look. I could see her whole face now, and there was no mistaking it. Angel! Walking along the high street, looking really tired and thin. I just hoped we could do something to help her.

* * *

The next morning, Soph and Abs arrived at my house bright and early.

'Are the girls here?' Nan trilled as I let them in.

'Yes, Nan,' I called back, with a pretty good idea of what was coming next.

Nan trundled out into the hall, her slippers making a flip-flap noise on the floor.

'Hi, Nana Parker,' said Soph.

'Hello, Mrs P,' said Abs.

She beamed at them. 'Morning, girls. Now, how about a nice cup of tea and a biscuit before you set off?'

'We're fine, Nan,' I said.

'Sure I can't tempt you?' she said. 'I've got a lovely packet of custard creams in the cupboard. Nothing like a nice custard cream.'

'No, thanks, Nana Parker,' said Soph, stifling a giggle.

'I'll just have to save them for *Inspector Morse*, then,' said Nan, flip-flapping back into the kitchen.

'Who's he?' whispered Abs.

'One of her TV detective shows,' I explained. Nan's got enough mystery books and DVDs to open a shop. I was pretty sure that with me and Mum out all day, she was planning a total TV-fest.

'Hi, girls.' It was Mum. I looked up and cringed. She was bounding down the stairs wearing legwarmers, a lemon-yellow ra-ra dress and a totally hideous stripy headband.

'She's going to a rehearsal,' I mumbled, wondering why my mum was so much more embarrassing than Soph's or Abs's. Luckily, they know all about Mum being in this seriously cringeworthy Bananarama tribute band, called the Banana Splits. It more or less explained this morning's disaster-zone of an outfit, even though I don't know why she can't wear normal clothes on the way to the rehearsal and change when she gets there. I mean, what if anyone from school saw her in that stuff when I was in the car? 'Oh, look, there's Rosie Parker – and that must be her mum, Borehurst's resident eighties throwback.'

'We've got a gig tonight,' Mum told Abs and Soph, proudly. She's so not cool enough to get away with using that word. 'I can still make time to give you a lift to the hospital though.' She winked. My public don't need me just yet.'

Oh, joy. Not only are her clothes crazy, she's actually lost her marbles, too.

'Let's go,' I said, desperate to get it over with.

'Have you got everything?' said Mum.

'Camera phone,' said Abs, pulling it out of her jeans pocket. 'And Teen Shimmer make-up bag.'

'Me, too,' I said, holding mine up.

'And,' said Soph, unzipping her Teen Shimmer bag and whipping out a chunky black pen, 'a marker, just in case Angel needs one to sign our bags.'

'I was thinking more along the lines of your bus fare home,' said Mum. 'Even Angel's autograph isn't going to get you very far on a number thirty-eight.'

* * *

Half an hour later, we pulled up outside Borehurst General Hospital. Even if we hadn't been excited about seeing Angel, it would have been a huge relief. Mum had spent the whole journey playing her favourite eighties songs in a feeble attempt to convince us that music was better back then. As if.

'"Careless Whisper",' Mum sighed as yet another of her favourites started playing. 'Now *that* is a great song.'

I opened the car door, ready to make my escape.

'They don't make them like that any more,' I mouthed to Abs and Soph behind Mum's back.

'They don't make them like that any more,' said Mum, shaking her head sadly.

'See you, Mrs Parker.' Soph clambered out of the car behind me, trying not to laugh.

'Thanks for the lift,' said Abs, getting out on the other side.

'Have fun,' Mum called after us. The car roared off with the sound of Mum's duet with George Michael wafting through the open window.

'Wow,' said Soph.

'I know,' I said. 'Seriously cringe-issimo.'

'Not that.' Soph elbowed me in the ribs, and I turned round to see what she was gawping at. 'This.'

'Sacré bleu!'

It looked as if the whole town had shown up to see Angel (apart from murder-mystery nutters and Bananarama maniacs, that is). There were people swarming everywhere.

'I didn't know Angel had so many fans,' I said.

'She's a local hero,' Soph declared. 'Our very own superstar.'

'Yeah, either that or they've been reading the gossip pages and want to see if the rumours are true,' said Abs, the cynic.

When it comes to killing a convo stone dead, no one does it quite like my mate, Abs.

'Anyway,' I said eventually. 'I suppose we should go and find a place to stand.'

Abs nodded. 'Somewhere we can get a good view.'

'And have the best chance of getting Angel's autograph,' said Soph.

We started making our way through the crowd. I kept seeing people I knew – little groups of girls from school, Mrs Campbell from the newsagent's and a couple of people who worked at the council offices with Mum.

'Look,' said Abs, grabbing my arm and pointing at a nearby figure. 'It's Time Lord!'

Our drama teacher, Mr Lord, is known as

Time Lord to everyone – except probably his mum. As he's so fond of telling us, he played a Cyberman in the original series of *Doctor Who* and this, in his deranged little brain, qualifies him as an expert on being famous.

'Rosie, celebrities are just normal people,' he once said when he found me reading *Star Secrets* instead of learning lines. 'They're as ordinary as you are. Nothing to get excited about.'

Which made it all the more hilarious to see him here, wearing an Angel T-shirt and carrying a dark red notebook, which very clearly had the word 'Autographs' written on the front in curly lettering.

'Watch,' I muttered to Soph and Abs. I stood on tiptoe so there was no way he could miss seeing me. Waving, I shouted really loudly, 'Hi, Mr Lord.'

He turned round, caught sight of me and jumped a mile. Under his sticky-up grey hair, his face went really red and he sort of half-waved before ducking down and hurrying off. We nearly died laughing.

As well as Time Lord and all the normal people, there were loads of photographers and journalists milling about. I recognised a few from local newspapers – Meanie Greenie, our beloved (not) headmistress is always inviting them to things like Sports Day and the end-of-term play, so she can humiliate us in print as well as real life – but you could so tell that most of them were from the national tabloids. The photographers had massive, expensive-looking cameras and they had all expertly shoved their way to the front of the crowd.

'It's nearly time,' said Abs, checking her watch anxiously.

'Follow me,' I told the girls, struck by a good idea. We slipped past a group of year-eight boys and two women waving Angel flags, and fell into step just behind one of the photographers. He had a shaved head, half an ear missing and he was truly enormous. Seriously, his bum was about as wide as me, Abs and Soph put together. He was making his way towards the metal barrier that separated the crowd from the front of the new hospital building. Big as he was, no one put up much of a fight as he made his way past. All we had to do was stick close behind him. Within a few minutes, we were right at the front of the crowd.

'Good thinking, Batgirl,' said Soph.

'Just call me a genius,' I grinned.

Now we were at the front, it was much easier to see what was happening. The new bit of the hospital was long and thin with this really cool glass entrance and a green and purple spiral pattern on the floor inside. A sign over the top read 'Welcome to the Children's Wing' and there was a wide, red ribbon right across the front. Next to it was a small, raised platform with a microphone on it. Five or six people in dark suits were walking around with mobiles and clipboards.

As we wriggled our way along the front of the barrier, I spotted the mayor strolling towards the platform, carrying a pair of ridiculously big scissors.

'What's he doing here?' said Soph. She sounded a bit panicky. 'You don't think Angel's ill and he's the last-minute replacement, do you?'

'No,' I said. 'Frankie would've texted us if she wasn't coming. He's probably –'

But just then I was distracted by a horribly familiar voice that made the end of the sentence drop right out of my brain.

'Of course, we were so close when she was at Whitney High,' said Amanda Hawkins. 'Jenny, as I still call her, was like a sister to me.'

All three of us whipped round to see just who Amanda was talking – OK, lying through her teeth – to.

'He must be a journalist,' muttered Abs as we all stared at the weasel-faced man who was standing next to Amanda, holding up a tiny voice-recorder.

'I'm hoping to model myself, or maybe act,' Amanda simpered, turning to a different journalist, this time a woman, on her other side. 'Jenny's promised to introduce me to her agent, because we're such good friends . . .'

'The lying witch,' hissed Soph. 'After what she did to Frankie. And as if someone as sweet as

Angel would ever be friends with Amanda Hawkins anyway.'

'No *way* should she get away with that,' I stormed. 'I'm going over there to set those journos straight about a few things.'

'Wait!' said Abs. 'I think that's Frankie's mum's car.'

A sleek, silver car had just pulled up alongside the hospital building. Me, Abs and Soph held our breath. The rest of the crowd gradually seemed to realise something was about to happen, too, because the breath-holding spread from us at the front right to the back, like a kind of Mexican wave of quietness. Then the car door opened. Angel stepped out gracefully and the crowd went bananas.

'It's her!' screamed Soph at the top of her voice. 'Angel!' She held up her phone and snapped a photo as Angel waved to the crowd.

My phone! I'd almost forgotten I had it. I fumbled in my pocket and pulled it out.

'She looks amazing!' Soph shouted.

'I know.' I couldn't stop grinning. OK, so we were there to solve a mystery, but it was really exciting to see Angel. I clicked away with my camera as she walked over to the platform, still waving.

The mayor spoke into the microphone. 'Ladies and gentlemen.' It took a few minutes, but eventually the noise died away. 'Ladies and gentlemen,' he repeated, 'it is my great pleasure to welcome back to Borehurst one of our most admired citizens, Miss Jenny Gabriel.'

The crowd, including me, Soph and Abs, roared our approval.

'Miss Gabriel – or Angel, as she's better known – will now perform our opening ceremony,' the mayor continued.

There was a bit of fussing as they both climbed down from the platform and posed in front of the ribbon for the photographers, who were going BONKERS clickety-clicking their cameras. There were more pics as the mayor handed Angel the comedy scissors and then one of his flunkies passed her a microphone.

'Thanks for such a fantastic welcome,' said Angel, smiling. 'It's great to be home.'

We all cheered loudly again and a man standing right behind us shouted, 'We love you, Angel!'

'I pronounce the Borehurst Hospital Children's Wing open,' she said, and cut the ribbon. She shook the mayor's hand and I held my phone up to snap a few more photos.

'Quick!' said Soph. 'Get your make-up bags out. She's coming over.' She held her silver Teen Shimmer bag over the barrier and popped the top off her marker pen.

Soph was right. The mayor had finally let go of Angel's hand and she'd come across to the front of the crowd to sign autographs.

'Angel!' Soph shouted again.

Abs grinned at me.

'Angel!' all three of us shouted.

She looked up and smiled at us.

'Oh, wow,' said Soph in a very high, squeaky voice.

'I think she's recognised us,' I croaked.

'She's heading right this way,' said Abs and even her sensible voice sounded a bit strange.

But as Angel walked towards us, I noticed she looked a bit unsteady on her feet. At first I thought it might be a high-heel thing, but she was wearing sparkly ballet pumps. She kind of swayed, lost her balance, and at the exact moment she reached our bit of the barrier, collapsed on the ground in front of us.

Chapter Four

If we'd thought the crowds and photographers were crazy before, it was nothing to the chaos that broke out now. People all around us shouted Angel's name and screamed. The photographers and journalists surged forwards, squashing me, Abs and Soph flat against the barriers, which were threatening to give way. The people at the back of the crowd were pushing, too, trying to see what was going on.

In front of us, Angel lay totally still on the ground. The mayor dashed over to her, followed by his assistants.

'Oi!' shouted the huge photographer we'd followed to the front of the crowd. 'Move. We can't see her.'

'Pig!' shouted Abs. 'As if that's what's important.'

'How can they take photos of her lying there?' I said.

Soph looked close to tears. 'Why isn't anyone helping her?'

But as we watched, the mayor took off his ceremonial cloak and spread it over her.

'She must be kept warm,' I heard him tell one of the assistants. 'Go over to the main hospital and fetch a doctor,' he ordered another. 'I'll stay here with Miss Gabriel. Bring me that microphone.' His voice was calm but firm and the assistants followed his orders in a flash of gleaming mobiles and sharp suits. The microphone arrived and the mayor stood up, leaving one of his assistants with Angel.

'Ladies and gentlemen,' announced the mayor again. 'Please remain calm. Angel has simply fainted. There is no immediate cause for concern.'

One of the assistants went over and whispered in the mayor's ear.

'I've just been informed that a doctor has been called,' the mayor continued, 'but there's no cause for alarm. For the time being, I would ask that you move back to give Angel some space and, once again, please keep calm.'

'Blimey,' said Abs. 'He's not the sort of bloke you'd argue with, is he?'

Me and Soph grinned, feeling a bit better. At least things were under control and help was on the way for Angel.

'She's probably just faking it,' came a spiteful voice from the crowd.

Amanda Hawkins. Quelle surprise.

'It's been going on for years,' she said, talking to the weasel-faced man again. 'She's always doing stuff for attention – y'know, like pretending to faint.' She turned to another journalist, who was scribbling all her lies down in his notepad.

'That's totally untrue, and you know it,' said Soph, glaring fiercely at Amanda.

'Yeah,' said Abs, 'the press make stuff up all the time – they don't need your help.'

'I can't stand this,' I said. The idiot photographers were still snapping gazillions of pics of Angel, the journalists with their microphones and notepads kept shouting her name, as if the first thing she'd do when she came round was talk to them, and now Amanda No-brain Hawkins was lying her bum off again.

Soph gave me a hug, and Abs joined in.

'It's totally horrible,' Soph agreed.

'It must be even worse for Frankie,' said Abs. She was looking over at the glass entrance to the Children's Wing. Mr and Mrs Gabriel came running out, with Frankie following close behind them. All three were making their way over to Angel, when we heard a shout. Two doctors in white coats rushed round the corner, with one of the mayor's assistants trying to keep up with them.

'Over here!' called Frankie's mum.

In an instant, Angel was surrounded by officials: the doctors, the mayor, two more of his assistants, Mr and Mrs Gabriel and Frankie. The photographers started pushing and shoving again, annoyed they couldn't see Angel.

One of the doctors ran inside the hospital and, before we knew it, paramedics were lifting Angel on to a stretcher and carrying her away. Soph looked like she might cry again. Angel's parents stood up and Mrs Gabriel put her arm round Frankie, who had tears streaming down her face. As they walked past, Frankie caught sight of us.

'I really hope she's OK,' I said, reaching over the barrier to squeeze Frankie's hand.

Frankie sniffed but looked kind of glad we were there. 'I'll text you as soon as we know anything,' she said.

We got the bus back to my house after that because we didn't know what else to do.

'I just can't stop thinking about poor Angel,' said Soph.

'I know. And we didn't find out anything useful,' I said. 'Unless the mayor's behind it all.'

'An evil genius, masterminding the downfall of

a beautiful young model . . .' said Abs, dreamily.

Me and Soph gave her this what-are-you-on-about look and she shut up.

'It's just us, Nan,' I yelled as we let ourselves in.

'You're home early,' she said, poking her head out of the lounge. 'Did you get to meet Fairy?'

What the crusty old grandads!.

'Her name's *Angel*,' I said. Very patiently, considering.

We went and sat on the sofa and told Nan everything that had happened at the hospital.

'That's just dreadful,' she said, when we'd finished. 'The poor lamb. And you three – all that excitement.' She shook her head and tutted. 'Tea. That's what you need. It's good for shock. And some biscuits. A nice cup of tea and a couple of my custard creams. Lovely!'

For once, we didn't argue. It was quite nice to be fussed over – besides which, I was starving. Mum had been practising this majorly annoying Bananarama song called 'I Heard A Rumour' at breakfast and it had put me right off my cereal.

We took the tea and biscuits upstairs to my room, leaving Nan puzzling over an episode of *Diagnosis Murder*.

* * *

'I can't even concentrate on gossip,' said Soph, ten minutes later. She shut the old issue of *Star Secrets* she'd been reading and flopped back on my bed, her head dangling upside down over the end.

'Doesn't that make you dizzy?' I said.

'Au contraire, mon frère. All the blood rushes to your head and it makes your hair totally shiny.'

'Where did you get that idea?' said Abs, who was standing in front of my mirror, messing with a pile of accessories.

Soph did a sort of upside-down shrug. 'Read it somewhere.'

'After the last few days, I'm going to stop believing everything I read,' I said, thinking of Angel again. Not that any of us had really stopped thinking about her.

'Is this the new Mirage song?' said Soph. We

had the radio on, but not too loud, to make sure we'd hear the phone if Frankie rang.

'Oui, oui,' I said, perking up a bit. 'It's good, no?'

'Très bon,' Soph agreed.

'What's this?' said Abs. She held up a weird, pink stretchy thing.

Oh, bum.

'Mum gave it to me,' I said cringing. She had been trying to convince me these things called snoods were coming back into fashion and I hadn't got round to throwing it away.

Abs stretched it out a bit, then tried to put it on as if it was a tube-top.

'Oh, for the love of giant sunglasses,' said Soph, sitting up. 'It's a snood. Give it here.'

'There's nothing you don't know about fashion, is there, Soph?' I said as she expertly twisted it into a sort of hat-scarf thing around Abs's head.

'Not much,' she admitted.

We studied Abs's reflection in the mirror.

'Yep.' Soph yanked the snood off. '*Sooo* never coming back into fashion.'

'Not even with a Sophie McCoy makeover?' Abs had an evil glint in her eye. Soph does this amazing thing where she takes old clothes – even disgusting, flowery, granny stuff from the charity shop – cuts them up, sews them back together and turns them into totally cool designer originals. Mostly, her stuff's brilliant, but sometimes it's just plain weird. There was no way she could ignore that challenge.

'Hmm, maybe I could do something with it.'

I was about to join in with Abs's game of Let's Wind Up Soph when something on the radio caught my attention.

'. . . Model, Angel, collapsed during the opening of a new wing at the hospital in her home town of Borehurst this morning.'

'Ssshhh!' I said, lurching across the room to turn up the volume.

'The news we're getting here is that she was rushed to the hospital's intensive-care unit,' said the DJ, 'and our sources tell us she's seriously ill. There's no official word from Angel's people yet, but we hear her condition's been caused by a nasty reaction to Teen Shimmer make-up. The range has been recalled from all shops and Teen Shimmer are urging customers not to use any products they have at home while an investigation is launched. Our fashion correspondent, Evie Alexander, is outside the hospital. What can you tell us, Evie?'

'Well, it's been a difficult day for both Angel and Teen Shimmer,' the fashion correspondent said. 'Experts say that not only is this disastrous for the country's most popular teen make-up range, but it could also spell the end of Angel's modelling career. Coupled with recent bad publicity over her health, the face of Teen Shimmer may well see bookings dry up as fast as a tube of mascara with the lid left off. Back to you in the studio, Ben.'

'Thanks, Evie. We'll be right back after these ads.'

I turned the radio down again as the stupid ad jingles started playing.

'No way is Teen Shimmer making Angel ill,' I scowled. It was impossible.

Me, Abs and Soph LOVE Teen Shimmer. I've got nearly every lipgloss in the whole range and, when we hit the mall, the Teen Shimmer counter is always the first place we go.

'Something is making her sick, though,' said Abs. 'You heard what he said. "Seriously ill." What d'you think they're doing about it?'

'She's in hospital,' said Soph. 'My dad always says you're in the best hands there.'

'Poor Frankie,' I said.

We all went quiet for a bit then, thinking about how she must be feeling.

'The thing is,' I said after a while. 'If it isn't Teen Shimmer, what *is* wrong with her? People don't just get ill for no reason.'

It didn't make any sense.

Chapter Five

My phone beeped and we all jumped. I grabbed it off my desk and opened the text message. It was from Frankie:

> Angel v. ill. Don't know what 2 do.
> Nightmare.

Abs and Soph read it over my shoulder.

'What should we send back?' said Abs.

'I wish there was something we could do to make her feel better,' said Soph, fiddling absentmindedly with the snood again.

'There is,' I said. 'Let's go and see her.'

Abs frowned. 'At the hospital?'

'No, Abs, in the country-music section at Top Choonz,' I said. 'Of course at the hospital.'

'Soph,' said Abs in a dignified sort of voice, 'will you ask the Great Sarcasmo just what she thinks we can do at the hospital?'

'Be there for Frankie,' I said. 'She really needs her friends at the moment.'

'And that's all?' said Abs, suspiciously.

Why do your friends always know what you're thinking, even when you try to pretend you're not thinking it at all? It is so annoying.

'OK, so it's not the *only* reason,' I admitted. 'But what's wrong with wanting to see if we can find anything out? We might be able to help.'

'There's no point arguing with her,' Soph told Abs. 'And seeing us might make Frankie feel a bit better.'

Abs sighed. 'Fine. But text her back so she knows we're coming.'

We caught the bus back to the hospital, stopping off on the way to buy some flowers and a card. Soph said you couldn't turn up to visit someone in hospital without taking flowers or grapes or something.

When Nan went into Borehurst General to have her ingrowing toenails done, all her mates from the library and the café and the community centre gave her stuff. She had so many flowers when she came home, Mum got hay fever and couldn't sing for a week.

I must find out if ingrowing toenails are painful and how you catch them.

There were more photographers and journalists than ever hanging around outside the hospital. They were blocking the whole entrance, and when we tried to get past them, they ignored us.

After about fifty goes, Abs got really narky.

'EXCUSE ME!' she shouted in the ear of this journalist, who was wearing a shiny leather jacket.

'Are you a friend of Angel's?' he asked her, practically dribbling at the idea he might have landed a scoop.

Abs looked disgusted. 'No,' she snapped. 'I'm a person trying to get into the hospital.'

The man shrugged. Looking majorly disappointed, he turned his back on her.

'Right,' I said. 'Soph, your Teen Shimmer bag, please.'

Soph, who carried the bag pretty much everywhere she went, gave it to me with a confused expression. I unzipped it and peered inside.

'Aha!'

'What are you – ' Abs began.

'Stand still,' I ordered as I took the top off Soph's Teen Shimmer Ultraviolet eye pencil.

'Hey!' she protested. OK, I *was* drawing spots all over her face and hands with it, but the situation was desperate.

'Voilà!' I stood back to admire Abs's face.

'How do I look?' she asked.

'Diseased.'

'Nice,' said Abs.

I grabbed one of her arms. 'Hold the other one, Soph,' I said, 'and try to hide the flowers.'

With me and Soph on either side of Abs, holding her up, we walked back towards the hospital entrance.

'Make way! Move, please!' I shouted as we walked. A few of the photographers turned round. 'Infectious disease coming through!'

More heads turned and some of them started backing away from us.

'This girl needs to see a doctor before the boils spread to the rest of her body,' I said.

'Aaargh,' groaned Abs for extra effect.

'Stand back!' yelled one of the photographers, leaping out of our way.

The rest of them seemed to think he had the right idea and a gap opened up. As we walked through, trying seriously hard not to laugh, I noticed there were a few television cameras trained on the entrance.

'If I end up on TV looking like this . . .' Abs hissed at me.

But we'd finally made it to the entrance.

'What now?' said Soph, looking around.

There was a huge map of the hospital on the wall opposite us, but I suddenly realised we had no idea where Angel was.

'We'll have to ask,' I said.

The reception desk was next to the giant map. I cleverly deduced this from the sign on the front that said 'reception desk'. A chunky woman with a sour face sat behind the desk, watching us.

'Hi,' I smiled. 'Can you tell me where to find Angel – I mean, Jenny Gabriel?'

She narrowed her eyes, suspiciously.

'We're friends of hers,' I said. 'Well, friends of her sister.'

'Yes, and I'm the Queen of Sheba,' said the receptionist.

Honestly, how come grown-ups are allowed to get away with sarcasm, but when I do it, I end up grounded or in detention?

'We'll just have to text Frankie and ask her,' said Soph.

'Good plan, Stan,' I said.

'Not in here you don't,' said the Queen of

Sheba, and pointed at a 'no mobile phones' sign above her throne.

FAN-BLOOMING-TASTIC.

'Listen, lady,' said Abs, leaning on the desk and waggling her finger.

The receptionist rolled backwards on her wheelie chair.

'Abs,' I said.

'Rosie, I can handle this.' She turned back to the nurse. 'We're here to see Frankie Gabriel, and if you don't tell us where she is . . .'

'I'm here,' said Frankie. We all turned round.

'Yes,' said Abs, backing down. 'Well.'

'Er, Abs,' said Frankie. 'What's up with your face?'

Abs put her hand up to her face and you could practically hear her thinking. She looked at the receptionist, who still seemed kind of horrified, and then at me and Soph. Yep. Still got the spots.

'Why didn't you remind me?' she asked.

'I tried!'

'It's a long story,' Soph told Frankie. She

handed Abs a face wipe and we headed out of the entrance hall, following Frankie.

'So how's Angel doing?' I asked.

Frankie shook her head. 'We don't really know. Doctors keep rushing in and out, but they always say they've got to do more tests.'

'We brought her a card,' said Soph. 'And some flowers.'

'Thanks,' said Frankie, trying to smile. 'She's not allowed any visitors, though. Mum's been in, and I went once, but there are all these tubes and wires and machines round her.'

She started sobbing. You could tell she'd hardly stopped all day. Her eyes were red and puffy and when she talked she sounded like she had a bad cold.

We stopped outside a set of double doors. Still crying, Frankie pushed them open. Inside was a small waiting room with squashy seats along two sides and a window looking through into another room. Frankie's mum was there. She looked just as awful as Frankie.

'Mum, these are my friends,' said Frankie. 'This is Rosie, Sophie and that's Abs.'

'Hi,' I said. 'We're all so sorry about Angel.'

'We brought these for her, for when she's feeling better,' said Soph, handing over the flowers and card.

'Sit down,' said Mrs Gabriel. 'It's so nice of you to come.'

We sat on the squashy seats.

'Frankie really needs her friends at the moment. We're all very worried.' Mrs Gabriel's voice cracked and her eyes filled with tears.

'We want to do whatever we can to help,' I said.

'Haven't they told you anything yet?' asked Soph, quietly.

Frankie shook her head. 'They're just doing tests all the time.'

'We won't know the results for a day or two,' said Mrs Gabriel.

'It would be bad enough if she was just ill,' Frankie burst out. 'But the paparazzi and the press won't leave her alone.'

'They were camping outside her flat in London,' Mrs Gabriel explained. 'We thought she could get away from them if she came back here for a few days, but they followed her. I suppose you saw the papers this morning?'

There was a stack of newspapers on the table. I picked one up and read the headline on the front:

FALLEN ANGEL

Underneath it was a photo of Angel looking seriously skinny. Even though the pic was in black and white, you could tell she was really pale, and her normally gorgeous hair was limp and straggly.

The other papers in the stack all had similar photos and headlines:

ANGEL: AN UNHOLY MESS

IS ANGEL GABRI-WELL?

'It's as if they want her to look as bad as possible, to get even more ill, so they can keep writing their nasty stories,' said Mrs Gabriel.

'Yeah, well they've got what they wanted,' said Frankie. 'One of the nurses put the TV on earlier, and all the news reports kept going on and on about overworked models and what a terrible company Teen Shimmer is. The papers tomorrow are going to be even worse.'

'Jenny's modelling agency really look after her though,' said Mrs Gabriel. It sounded like she'd said it a gazillion times before. She had that tone in her voice my mum gets when she says, 'No, Rosie, you cannot have a DVD player in your bedroom'.

'And no way is Teen Shimmer to blame, either,' said Frankie. 'Angel gave me loads of the free make-up she got, and I'm OK.'

'If anyone was going to get ill from Teen Shimmer,' said Abs, 'it would be Soph. Have you seen the way she trowels it on when we go out?'

'Hey!' protested Soph, but she laughed along with the rest of us. It was kind of a relief, when everything else was so bad.

The double doors swung open and a woman in a white coat walked in.

'I'm here to do a few more tests on Jenny, Mrs Gabriel,' she said. 'I just need you to sign some forms.'

'We'd better go,' said Abs, and we all stood up.

'Text us if you find out anything else,' I said, hugging Frankie.

I stepped away so Abs and Soph could say goodbye to her, and noticed the woman in the white coat going into the room on the other side of the window. With a rush of horror, I suddenly realised it must be Angel's room. I could just make out a bed in the middle of all the machines and wires Frankie had talked about, and a thin figure lying perfectly still while everything blipped and beeped and whirred around her.

'I'll see you soon,' Frankie said, snapping me back into the conversation. We waved and walked out into the corridor.

'Did you see her?' I said. My voice sounded kind of shaky and shocked.

'Frankie?' said Abs, frowning. 'Of course we did.'

'No, Angel. In that other room – through the glass.'

Soph clapped a hand to her mouth.

'She was all wired up to machines. This is so serious.'

'I just don't get it,' said Abs. 'I mean, why can't they find out what's wrong with her?'

'And why isn't anyone trying to find out what's *really* going on?' I said. 'We have GOT to get to the bottom of this. I just wish I knew where to start.'

'We'll think of something,' said Abs.

* * *

When we got back to my house, we wrote the following list:

Five things we know for sure:

1. We just *have* to help Angel and Frankie.
2. Life's not worth living without Teen Shimmer. Therefore, we have to rescue the reputation of Teen Shimmer too.
3. Teen Shimmer IS NOT to blame for what's happened to Angel. We all use it. So do millions of other girls. None of us is sick.
4. Angel is not an overworked model.
5. The mayor is probably not to blame either.

OK, so it wasn't a very long list.

'We don't really know anything about Teen Shimmer,' I realised, sucking the end of my biro.

'Apart from the names of just about every lippy and eye shadow in the whole range,' said Soph. 'And that it totally rocks.'

'Well, duh. But how's that going to help?'

'No problemo,' said Abs. 'We just look it up on the Internet.'

I switched my computer on and fetched two extra chairs so we could all sit at my desk. Abs put her glasses on.

'OK,' I said, tapping away once the browser came up. 'T-e-e-n S-h-i-m-m-e-r. And "search".'

'Oooh, look!' said Soph, pointing at the screen as a list of results appeared. 'There's a half-price sale on all their lipglosses.'

'Focus, Soph,' said Abs. 'Scroll down a bit, Rosie.'

I moved further down the page, past loads more sites that were selling Teen Shimmer products, and then on to another page that was more or less the same.

'We're not finding out much, except that loads of shops sell it,' I said.

'Try searching "Teen Shimmer company information",' Abs suggested.

I typed it in.

'There!' I said. 'Their official website. That should have tons of useful stuff.'

I clicked on the link. There were pics of lipstick tubes and mascara wands, a list of shops that sold the range, some photos of models wearing it (including Angel) and this cool thing where you could click on a drawing of a face and add different Teen Shimmer make-up. We spent quite a long time researching that page.

'Nothing,' I said, opening the last page – 'Contact Us'.

'There's an address,' said Abs. 'Maybe we could go there to investigate?'

'Maybe,' I said. 'But it's miles away.'

'There must be something else,' said Soph.

I tried the search engine again, and we found a few more mentions of Teen Shimmer. They'd won a ton of beauty awards in magazines and sponsored this reality TV show called *Teen Tantrums*, but there was nothing that gave us any real clues or linked them to Angel's illness.

There was a knock on the door. As usual, my mum opened it before I even had chance to say 'come in'. One day I will get to grips with DIY and put a lock on it – then maybe she will learn.

'I'm just off to my gig now, girls,' she said.

Really, Mum? I thought you were nipping out to the corner shop in the dungarees, checked shirt and insanely large hair bow.

'Good luck,' said Soph.

'Actually,' – Abs checked her watch – 'I'd better go, too.'

'I'll give you a lift, if you like,' said Mum. 'You too, Soph?'

Soph looked at me. 'What about Angel?'

'Let's sleep on it,' I said. I didn't want to admit it, but I was stumped. Sans clue, as les Français would put it. I kind of hoped Abs might have one of her legendary brainwaves over night. 'We'll meet back here first thing tomorrow.'

'Aye, aye, Captain Parker,' said Soph, pulling on her jacket.

'Au revoir,' added Abs.

I slumped over my desk in shame as they trooped down the stairs, with Mum singing Bananarama songs at the top of her voice.

* * *

'Just you and me tonight, then,' said Nan, chirpily.

I'd gone downstairs to make myself some beans on toast. Mum was too busy being a Banana Split to feed her only child. Honestly, I'm practically an orphan thanks to the eighties.

'Why don't you pop that on a tray and eat it on the sofa with me?' said Nan. 'There's a lovely murder-mystery just about to start on TV.'

Oh, joy.

Is this really what my life has come to? Staying in on a Saturday night, eating baked beans and watching TV with a pensioner. Where are the parties and the sleepovers and the hordes of gorgey boys I should be snogging? Actually, just one boy would do. I'm not greedy.

Nan's show was one of those rubbish made-for-TV movies where everyone has huge hair that's almost as stiff as their acting. The two main characters were models, which kept reminding me of Angel.

'You know that advertising contract was mine,' screamed the girl with stiff ginger hair.

'I won it fair and square,' the girl with stiff blonde hair screamed back.

Ginger then whacked Blondie over the head with a paperweight and Blondie fell to the floor in a pool of blood.

Totally far-fetched. I mean, apart from anything else, how come the murder weapon didn't just bounce off her hairspray? And a paperweight? Pur-lease. When have you ever seen one, except on TV? The only thing anyone uses them for is committing murders.

Nan was gripped.

I pulled one of Mum's glossy mags off the

coffee table and started flipping through it. There was a picture of Angel in it, and I thought about texting Frankie to see if she had any more news or clues. She'd promised to call us though. Besides, I couldn't help feeling the doctors and tests weren't going to be the answer.

'That detective's ever so handsome,' said Nan, dreamily.

He was wearing white socks and had a moustache that looked like it was made of the stuff hamsters sleep in.

I got up off the sofa. 'I've just remembered there's some homework I need to finish,' I lied.

I was starting to understand what Soph's dad means when he says TV rots your brain.

Chapter Six

The next morning, Abs and Soph turned up at my house just like we'd agreed.

'So, what's the plan, Stan?' I asked Abs, sure she'd have come up with something brilliant by now.

'I thought we were going to have another look on the Internet,' she said, sounding a bit confused. 'You know, see if we can find out anything else about Teen Shimmer that might give us a clue.'

And that's it, is it? Le grand plan de Abs. And she's meant to be the brains of this outfit. Looks like it's all down to Rosie Parker again.

'Fine,' I sighed, and switched the computer on. It wasn't easy being brilliant.

'Rosie,' said Soph as we waited for the browser to pop up. 'What's that noise?'

All three of us looked up at the ceiling. It was a sort of scuffling sound.

'Mum,' I said. 'She's up in the attic.'

'Why?'

'She said she was tidying up. As if!' I snorted. 'I'd bet my MP3 player *and* my collection of *Star Secrets* magazines she's going through boxes of old clothes looking for stage costumes.'

'Clothes?' Soph's eyes lit up. 'I wonder if there's anything she doesn't want?'

She started drifting towards the door.

Abs grabbed her by the shoulders and yanked her back into the room.

'Sit,' she said, plonking Soph down in the chair next to me. 'You can worry about Rosie's mum's clothes later.'

'I spend half my life worrying about them,' I muttered.

'Both of you, concentrate.' Abs put her specs on and clicked on to the search engine. 'We've got work to do, remember – Angel? Teen Shimmer?'

It didn't take long for us to realise we'd already seen nearly all of the sites in the search results. As we got nearer to the bottom of the list, the info was less and less useful.

'Did you know,' I said, reading from a TV trivia website, 'Teen Shimmer make-up is sold at the corner shop in top Australian soap opera, *Hart Grove* and some of the stars use it in real life, too?'

'I did, actually,' said Soph.

I tried a few more links.

'Here's one that's got an interview with Teen Shimmer's head lipgloss designer,' I said. Abs and Soph leaned in so we could all read it together. But there was nothing that even began to explain what had happened to Angel.

'What about the news?' said Abs. 'Maybe one of those journalists buzzing around yesterday managed to find out something useful that could give us a clue.'

'Fat chance,' I said. 'All they want is the gory details on Angel. They don't care what's really wrong with her.'

'It could still be worth a try,' said Soph. 'We're probably not going to find out anything else here.'

'I think Nan might have today's paper,' I said.

But before I could go and fetch it from mystery-novel HQ, the doorbell rang.

'Can you get that, Rosie?' Mum's muffled voice shouted from the attic.

I was about to argue – it's always me who has to do the rubbish stuff, like answering the door and washing up – but I was going downstairs anyway and it never hurts to make Mum think I'm being cooperative. You never know when you might need something from your parent?

'Fine!' I yelled back up at her.

I ran downstairs and bumped into Nan in the hall.

'It's OK, Nan – I've got it.'

'If it's one of those conmen saying he needs to come in and check the gas, tell him I've got an alarm and a baseball bat,' said Nan.

I am officially the only sane person living in this house. I pulled the door open as Nan flip-flapped back to her books.

'Frankie! Come in!'

'Thanks.'

'What's up? Is Angel OK?'

Abs and Soph came crashing down the stairs. They'd obviously been listening from the landing.

'She's not worse, is she?' asked Soph.

Frankie shook her head. 'She's still the same. Mum said I needed to get out of the hospital for a while. I just thought I'd come and see if you'd found anything out,' said Frankie.

There was an awkward silence. I bit my lip, feeling worse than ever that we hadn't got a single piece of useful information yet.

'I'm really sorry,' I said. 'We've looked everywhere we can think of.'

'We've been to hundreds of websites, but . . . nothing,' said Abs, shaking her head.

'There has to be something we're missing,' I

said. 'Something really obvious – a clue we already know about, but just don't know it's a clue.'

'Let's start with what we do know,' Abs suggested.

I nodded. 'OK. Angel's lost loads of weight and she keeps fainting, but she's definitely looking after herself properly.'

'And she's not on drugs,' said Frankie. We must have looked shocked, because she explained, 'That's what one of the papers said this morning.'

'She's the face of Teen Shimmer, but it's not that either,' said Soph. 'We know because none of us is ill, and nor is anyone else who uses it.'

'What did you find out about Teen Shimmer?' asked Frankie.

I counted off on my fingers. 'Their head lipgloss-designer is a woman called Sarah something-or-other, they don't do any animal testing, they've been the biggest make-up brand in the country for two years running and there's a new range of colours coming out this month.'

'There's your answer!' said a voice. It was Nan.

She'd obviously been earwigging from the lounge. Whatever happened to privacy, that's what I want to know?

'Hello, dear,' she said, turning to Frankie. 'I'm Rosie's Nan. You must be Fairy's sister.'

'ANGEL!' all four of us said.

'Yes, Angel,' said Nan. 'How is she?'

Frankie started to look a bit damp around the eyes again. 'It's pretty serious,' she said.

'Oh, dear.' Nan patted Frankie's hand. 'It's a good job you've got Rosie on the case.'

'Yeah, big help I am,' I mumbled. 'Hang on, Nan. What did you mean before, "there's your answer"?'

'Like you said, you've got all the information you need.'

'But we haven't. None of it makes any sense.'

Nan tutted. 'It's just like in the film last night.'

Nope. Still not a clue what she's going on about.

'Did you see it?' she asked the others. '*Dead Beautiful*. There was this ever-so-handsome detective. He solved the case even though he was heartbroken, because he'd secretly been in love with the victim.'

'Nan,' I said, warningly.

'I *knew* you weren't paying attention,' she said. 'Now, think. Who was the killer?'

'The model with the ginger fright-wig.'

'Savannah-May,' said Nan. 'Yes. Who did she kill?'

'The other one. The blonde model.'

'Montana,' said Nan.

I was beginning to suspect my mum got off quite lightly being called Elizabeth.

'And why did Savannah-May kill Montana?'

'Because they were rivals,' I said.

'There you go!' said Nan, as if she'd just handed me the solution to world peace or something.

'You mean,' said Abs, slowly, 'Angel's got a rival?'

'Someone who thinks *they* should be the face of Teen Shimmer?' I said, remembering how Ginger thought she should have got Blondie's job in the film.

'No,' said Frankie. 'There wasn't anyone else up for the job. Angel was the only one they wanted.'

'Maybe it isn't about her,' Nan suggested. 'It could be the make-up company. They might have a rival.'

I rolled my eyes at the others, without Nan seeing. I mean, that film was *sooo* far-fetched.

'It couldn't hurt to find out, I guess,' said Frankie. She looked really sad and desperate. You'd have to be pretty sad and desperate to take your lead from one of Nan's murder shows, if you ask me.

'Lovely,' said Nan, and we all went up to my bedroom while she trotted off in search of custard creams, or garibaldis or something.

* * *

'Teen Shimmer rivals', I typed. The others watched over my shoulder as a screen full of results came up.

'Glam Girls,' said Abs, pointing at the screen.

The name was in about five of the results.

'Ew,' said Soph. 'Their stuff's seriously bad.'

'I've never heard of them,' said Frankie.

'They used to be big,' Soph told us, 'but then Teen Shimmer came along and it's loads better.'

'Amanda Hawkins uses it,' I said, remembering something. 'I came out of the girls' toilets behind her one day and I nearly choked to death on her perfume. It was Glam Girls.'

'Quick,' said Abs. 'Look up their website.'

I did another search and found it straight away. When the site opened, the front page had this huge picture of the woman who ran Glam Girls. 'Lysanne Rogers, Chief Executive', according to the caption underneath the photo. Something clicked in my brain. I'd seen her somewhere before.

'Does her face look familiar to you?' I said.

'Nope,' said Abs.

'I don't think so,' said Frankie.

'Even if it did, I'd never admit I knew someone who dressed like that,' said Soph.

'I *know*,' Abs giggled. 'And look at some of these make-up names. Twinkle Toes Pink. Perfect Peach. Lovely Lavender. YUK!' She mimed being sick. Even Frankie was giggling.

My brain was buzzing.

'Anyone hungry?' I said.

'Always,' said Soph. 'What've you got?'

'Cupcakes and banana smoothies,' I said. Mum had gone shopping first thing after I moaned about the baked beans I'd had for dinner, so the fridge was full of proper snacks for once.

'Yum,' said Soph. 'Need any help, amigo?'

'Non, merci.'

'We'll stay here and see what else we can find out,' said Abs, sliding into my chair as I left the room.

I went downstairs, thinking hard. *Lysanne Rogers.* Nope, it wasn't her name I recognised, it was definitely her face. I tried to remember where I might have seen her. It wasn't at school, or anywhere in town. She wasn't someone Mum worked with, or Nan had tea with in Trotters, the café on the high street. I grabbed a plate for the cupcakes. Maybe she'd been in *Star Secrets*, or on TV?

YES! That was it. TV . . . But it couldn't be.

Lysanne Rogers looked just like the make-up artist from this documentary I'd seen about Angel a few weeks before. And now I thought about it, she was there at the hospital too. I saw her in the crowd at the opening of the children's wing. I'd sort of recognised her then, but just thought she was there to do Angel's make-up. The question – the really big question – was why would Lysanne Rogers be working as a make-up artist, or pretending to be one? And, what, exactly, would the Chief Executive of Glam Girls be doing at the opening of a children's hospital in boring Borehurst?

Eight possible reasons for Lysanne Rogers to be at the hospital:

1. She really cares about sick children. (Yeah, right.)

2. She wants people to *think* she really cares about sick children.
3. She thinks sick children should wear more make-up.
4. She was trying to sell make-up to sick children's rellies, who always look a bit on the pale side.
5. She was hoping to convince the hospital shop to stock make-up as well as grapes and stale chocolate.
6. She'd come to present Amanda Hawkins with the Biggest User of Too Much Glam Girls Perfume award.
7. She wanted Angel's autograph.
8. Or maybe . . .

SACRÉ BLEU! The plate I was holding slipped out of my hand and smashed on the kitchen floor. It was a horrible idea – a totally terrifying possibility – but it would explain *everything*.

Chapter Seven

'Hey,' said Soph, as I dashed back into the bedroom, 'what about the cakes?'

The three of them were still sitting in front of the computer, but I hardly noticed. My phone was on the window sill and I grabbed it, frantically stabbing at buttons until the photo gallery appeared. Flipping through the pics I'd taken at the hospital, I finally found the one I wanted. Squinting at the screen, I was pretty sure I could see Lysanne Rogers.

'Um, Rosie,' said Abs. 'What's going on?'

'Budge over,' I said, wriggling back into my chair. I sent the photo from my phone to the computer and then opened it up and zoomed in. Result! Not just Lysanne Rogers. Oh, no. Lysanne Rogers pulling a face that totally obviously said 'I hate Angel'. She so didn't know anyone was looking at her, let alone pointing a camera in her direction.

'It's her,' I said to the others. They all peered at the screen.

'Angel?' said Soph, looking at the foreground of the picture.

'No, Lysanne Rogers. From Glam Girls.' I pointed at the crowd.

'What's she doing there?' Abs wondered.

'And why did you take a photo of her?' asked Frankie.

'I didn't. Not on purpose, anyway.'

'What are you on about?' asked Abs.

I very patiently got up and sat cross-legged on the bed, ready to explain my brilliant deductions to them. This is how the conversation went:

Me: *So, you know how I told you I recognised her picture?*

Abs: *No. You just asked if we thought she looked familiar.*

Me: *Whatever.*

Soph: *Is that why you've forgotten the cakes?*

Me: *This isn't about cakes.*

Abs: *What is it about, then?*

Me: *SHUT UP! [Big pause.] So, I recognised Lysanne Rogers' picture, and I've remembered where I saw her. She was in that documentary about Angel the other week – she was her make-up artist.*

Soph: *But she isn't a make-up artist. She's the head of Glam Girls.*

Me: *I know. That's why it's so fishy. Anyway, then I remembered I'd seen her at the hospital as well.*

Abs: *Why would she be there?*

Me: *It's Nan's film, isn't it? The rivals. That's what got us here in the first place. Glam Girls and Teen Shimmer are rivals.*

Soph: *No way is Glam Girls a match for Teen Shimmer.*

Me: *Exactly. Teen Shimmer sells loads more, but if Lysanne Rogers can get rid of Teen Shimmer somehow . . .*

Abs: *Like, get all their make-up taken out of the shops . . .*

Me: *. . . then Glam Girls is the biggest make-up brand in the country. All Lysanne Rogers has to do is get to Angel and somehow make her ill, then start a rumour that Teen Shimmer is to blame. And voilà.*

Yes, yes, I know. I am a genius.

'Blimey,' said Abs, after a minute.

'Are you sure?' asked Soph. 'The photo shows she was at the hospital yesterday, but how do we know she's been anywhere near Angel?'

'The documentary,' I said. 'I'm *positive* it was her doing Angel's make-up.'

'There's one way to find out,' said Frankie. 'My mum keeps everything to do with Angel. She's got all the magazines and adverts she's done, and the TV stuff, too.' She rubbed the side of her nose, looking sort of embarrassed. 'It's because she's really proud. I mean, Angel's so normal, but she's done all these amazing things.'

'Did she record the documentary?' I asked hopefully.

'Yep,' said Frankie. 'She had to go out when it was on, so I set the DVD for her. We've still got it.'

I jumped off the bed. 'What are we waiting for?'

* * *

Frankie's house was a bit weird. Between Mum's constant singing and Nan's TV shows, there's never a quiet moment at our house. Frankie's was dead quiet. You could sort of tell no one had been there for a few days and it was spooky – like the house knew something was going on.

'It's in here somewhere,' said Frankie. Me, Abs and Soph sat on the sofa as she looked through a box of DVDs with 'Angel' written on the front.

She turned on the TV and DVD player and popped a disc in, pressing play.

'This is it!' I said.

Frankie sat next to us with the remote. 'Can you remember which bit she was in?'

'I think it was about halfway through,' I said.

She pressed the fast-forward button and the film whizzed past at top speed for a minute or two.

'STOP!' I was sitting right on the edge of the sofa. 'There – I'm sure that was it. Go back a bit.'

Frankie moved the DVD back a few seconds, and then froze it as we caught a quick glimpse of Lysanne Rogers. There was no mistaking her face.

'Rosie, you're a legend,' said Soph. I tried very hard not to look smug.

'So, what do we do now?' asked Frankie.

I didn't answer, just sat there with my mouth hanging open in a goldfishy way. The thing was, I hadn't really thought past this bit. After not knowing anything, I was totally buzzing about working out what was going on. I haven't sat through, like, a thousand of Nan's detective shows without knowing the difference between 'whodunit' and 'whomighthavedunit'.

'I *know* it's her,' I said. 'It's got to be.'

'But we haven't exactly got any proof,' said Abs.

'What about this?' I pointed at the frozen TV screen. 'And my phone.'

'Circumstantial evidence,' said Abs. *Not just me watching those crime shows, then.*

'So, are we just meant to do nothing?' I asked.

'No way, José,' said Frankie. 'If that witch has done something to my sister, we've got to find out what it is, and how to make Angel better.'

'We could go to the Glam Girls office and look for evidence,' Soph suggested.

'They won't be open on a Sunday, and Mum'll kill me if I bunk off school tomorrow,' I said.

'Besides, how would we get there?' said Abs. 'The address on the website is in London.'

Frankie pushed her hands through her hair. It went all bonkers and sticky-out. 'We can't wait,' she said, desperately. 'If we don't do something, it could be too late for Angel.'

'What about the police?' I suggested. 'They could find Lysanne Rogers.'

'Yeah, right,' said Abs. 'Like the police will take any notice of us. They'll just think we've been watching too much TV.'

'So what?' said Soph. She turned the TV off and ejected the disc. 'It's the best plan we've got,' she said, now waggling the disc at us. 'If the police don't do anything about it, we'll just have to think of something else. It's not like they're going to make things worse, is it?'

It was all very un-Soph-ish. Instead of Soph, fashion guru, who's been sent home twice this term for wearing what Meanie Greenie calls 'inappropriate school attire', she was Super-Soph, all steely determination.

I looked round, first at Abs and then at Frankie, who seemed to be thinking the same thing as me.

PC Plod HQ here we come.

Mum: Where are U?
Me: On way 2 police station.

Mum: What?! Pls tell me U R joking.

Me: At least no handcuffs. :o)

Mum: Don't U :o) me. What's going on?

Me: Is Nan's fault. We solved Angel mystery!

Mum: Be home 4 tea, or will b a murder mystery.

Honestly, you never see Jessica Fletcher or Miss Marple getting nagged by their mum to come home halfway through a brilliant bit of detecting. Although Miss Marple is, like, a hundred, so her mum would be seriously wrinkle-issimo and probably not up for much tea-making. Maybe that's why there are so many unsolved crimes. Policemen and policewomen, just about to arrest the prime suspect, being dragged away from the crime scene because their mum's got cheese-on-toast waiting.

'Well, this is it,' said Soph, as we got off the bus outside the police station. She sounded quite a bit less like steely determination Soph now we were actually there.

'Hey,' I said, having a sudden thought. 'You don't suppose Lysanne Rogers is still here do you? In Borehurst, I mean. Maybe she decided to hang around and make sure everything went to plan with Angel and Teen Shimmer and all those reporters.'

'We could go and find her,' said Soph.

'How?' said Abs. 'She could be anywhere.'

'It would still take too long,' Frankie pointed out. 'Besides, we're here now. We may as well go in.'

All four of us stood there, staring up at the big stone building. My stomach was churning, like the time I had to confess to Mum that I'd worn her Duran Duran sweatshirt and leggings to a fancy-dress party (I went as an old person) and someone had spilled blackcurrant all down the front. I took a deep breath.

'Come on then,' I said. The others followed me inside.

Despite my reputation as a total trouble magnet, I had never actually been inside Plod HQ before. The police took our statements after the

Mirage Mullins incident at Soph's house. The station (as it's called in police lingo) was so not impressive. It reminded me a bit of the council offices where mum works, or our doctor's surgery. On one side, there was a reception desk. Against the opposite wall, there was a hard-looking bench, probably for hard-looking suspects to sit on. The walls were covered in really rubbish posters saying things like, 'Lock up, or lose out!' and the whole place smelled like the stuff Nan uses on the bath when she's on one of her house-cleaning missions.

'Yes, ladies,' said a policeman, looking up as we walked in. 'What can we do for you?'

What, no 'ello, 'ello, 'ello?

'I – I mean, we,' I started, 'are here to report a crime.'

'A crime, eh?' He had this really stupid smirk on his face. Maybe Abs had been right.

'Yes,' I said. *Rise above his idioticness, Rosie.* 'We've got evidence that someone has been deliberately trying to make the model Angel ill, to destroy Teen Shimmer.'

'Have you now?' he said. Still smirking. Still, apparently, only able to talk in questions.

This was getting très annoying.

Before I said anything else, a door opened behind the desk and another policeman stuck his head out.

'Robinson, have you seen those keys?' he asked.

Smirky Robinson looked a bit flustered (ha!) and started hunting all round the desk. The other policeman turned and I realised I knew him. He'd interviewed us as Soph's house.

'The Mirage Mullins detectives!' He stepped right through the door now, held out his hand and shook first mine, then Abs's, Soph's and lastly, looking a bit confused, Frankie's. 'Sergeant Edwards,' he told us. 'Nice to see you again.'

'What? OW!' Smirky Robinson was bent down under the desk, still searching for the keys. Is it wrong to laugh when someone that annoying hits their head on a desk? No, it is not.

'You, er, keep looking, Robinson,' said Sergeant Edwards. 'I'll take care of things here. Now, what seems to be the problem, girls?'

I felt seriously relieved. Last time we'd met him, the sergeant had been so impressed with our detecting he'd told us we should think about joining the force when we left school. Like that's ever going to happen. But it meant he might just believe us about Lysanne Rogers.

I passed him the DVD and the photo we'd printed off from my phone and explained everything we'd found out about Angel, Teen Shimmer, Glam Girls and Lysanne Rogers. When I finished talking, he just stood there for a minute, looking like a stunned kipper.

'You worked all of this out by yourselves?' he eventually said.

'Yep.'

'Amazing. And I'm pleased you didn't go running off to accuse Ms Rogers yourselves this time.'

'We would've, but Glam Girls is too far away and tomorrow's a school day and it's all really urgent because Angel's so ill,' said Soph, who was back to her normal blabbermouth self.

'What she means,' – I glared at Soph – 'is, we thought if we came here, you'd be able to sort it out faster than us.'

'You do believe us, don't you?' said Frankie.

'Well, you've got a bit of a track record where this sort of thing is concerned. I reckon it's worth a few hours of police time to check out your story and try to track this Lysanne Rogers down.'

'She might still be in Borehurst,' I said. 'I mean, waiting around to check her plan's still working.'

'Leave it with me,' said the sergeant. 'I'll get Robinson here on the case.' He glanced at Robinson, who had dust all over his shoulders and a really gross red bump on his forehead from hitting his head on the desk. 'On second thoughts, maybe someone a bit more efficient,' said the sergeant.

Chapter Eight

By some amazing chance I got back before tea, so Mum didn't have to go to the trouble of killing me. Sergeant Edwards offered to drive us all home in his police car, but most of our neighbours already think I'm a crazed arsonist – thanks to the time I left a tea towel next to the oven and it accidentally caught fire – so I got the bus instead. When I walked in, there was this weird smell and the minute I went into the kitchen I realised why: Mum was cooking. Usually, she buys stuff that's dead easy to cook – pasta, chicken, jacket potatoes

– and she's pretty much OK at making it. Every so often, though, she gets this urge to cook something more complicated. Serious mistake. It always ends up burnt, or freezing cold in the middle, or just plain disgusting. And then there's the mess.

'Hello, love,' said Mum. 'How was the police station?'

She had flour in her hair and tomato sauce on one cheek. The kitchen looked like the kind of place you'd expect to see a news crew reporting from. You know, with a number on the bottom of the screen asking for donations to help rebuild the lives of the people who live there.

'Fine. I'm just going to go and, um . . .' I slowly backed out of the room.

I wandered into the lounge, sort of hoping by some miracle Nan wasn't there and I might be able to watch – oooh, I don't know – a programme that didn't include someone getting done in for once. Fat chance.

'I just thought I'd have a quick flick round with the duster while *Columbo*'s on,' she said. There was a cloud of dust and bits of feather from the duster hanging in the air.

What was the point? I stomped upstairs. Honestly, it was like being a prisoner, except instead of bars, I was confined to my room by a dust-bothering pensioner and a *Ready, Steady, Cook* reject.

It wasn't that I was in a bad mood exactly. I just felt a bit helpless, leaving the police to sort out the Angel situation. They didn't really care about it the way me, Abs and Soph did. Like Sergeant Edwards would be bothered if he couldn't buy a Shimmer No. 5 LipTube ever again!

I decided to try doing some homework. Yes, I was that desperate.

* * *

A few hours later, I'd done quite a bit. My hair was all washed and straightened, I'd checked *Star Secrets*, *Celebz.com* and Maff's blog, reorganised my CD collection and decided on a title for my geography essay. I was just about to start on the first paragraph (I was – honestly) when Abs instant-messaged me:

> **CutiePie:** Any news your end, amigo?
> **NosyParker:** Mum is cooking.
> **CutiePie:** Holy burnt offerings, Batgirl! Remember there's that emergency choccy bar in your school bag.
> **NosyParker:** Is sooo an emergency. Wish I knew what the police were doing.
> **CutiePie:** Did the sarge say he'd ring you?
> **NosyParker:** Non. He HAS to, though. Is only fair. It's *our* case!

I thought I'd try Soph and see if she knew anything:

> **NosyParker:** Have you heard from les plods?
> **FashionPolice:** Not a sausage.
> **NosyParker:** Me neither.

FashionPolice: Wonder how Angel is.

NosyParker: Oooh, must go. Phone's ringing.

'Rosie?'

It was Frankie.

'How's Angel?'

'She's going to be OK,' said Frankie. Her voice was shaking and she still sounded a bit snotty, but I could tell she was totally relieved. 'Everything's going to be OK. Sergeant Edwards was here, and it's all sorted.'

YESSS! I flopped back on my bed and kicked my trainers off.

'Spill.'

Frankie giggled. 'It only happened, like, an hour ago, but he turned up here at the hospital and told us they'd found Lysanne Rogers. She was staying at that hotel near to where Abs lives, and she wasn't using a false name or anything.'

'I bet she thought nobody would ever suspect her, or even know who she was.'

'That's what the police said! So anyway, they went there and took her for thingummy.'

'Took her in for questioning,' I said, helpfully. I am an expert on police lingo, thanks to Nan.

'Yes,' said Frankie. 'And when they got her back to the police station, she admitted everything straight away. She said Glam Girls was losing loads of money, all because of Teen Shimmer, and she was trying to put a stop to it.'

'She confessed, just like that?'

'Yep. Then they asked her about the documentary and posing as a make-up artist, and she admitted that, too. We only saw, like, a second of it on that film, but she's been working with Angel for ages and –' Frankie's voice went really shaky again. She took a deep breath. 'She was putting poison in the Teen Shimmer stuff she used on Angel.'

'You lie!' I said. 'That is *seriously* evil.'

'I know. But the good thing is, the police found out exactly what sort of poison it was and the doctors say it explains everything – losing so much weight, her spots, the fainting – all of it.'

'So, can they sort her out?' I kind of guessed they could or Frankie would be more upset.

'They can totally treat it,' she said. 'The antidote's already working. Mum reckons she'll be out of hospital by the end of the week.'

Am I good or what?

'We're all majorly grateful,' she said. 'I mean, you saved Angel's life. The doctors and the police and everyone say so.'

'Just doin' my job, ma'am,' I said in this silly deep voice.

Frankie laughed. 'Will you tell Soph and Abs and say thanks to them, too?'

'Do the French wear dodgy berets?'

✳ ✳ ✳

On Thursday afternoon, me, Abs and Soph went to visit Angel in hospital. Frankie had phoned again to say her sis was loads better and really wanted to see us. Amanda Hawkins went as green as a plate of sprouts when she found out.

This time, we walked straight past the sour-faced receptionist. When we reached the waiting room, there was no sign of Frankie or her mum.

'What do we do now?' said Soph. 'I mean, we can't just waltz into Angel's room. She's, like, a megastar.'

'Yeah, a megastar whose life we saved,' Abs argued.

'I think it's OK if we go in,' I said. Through the window, I'd just spotted Angel sitting up in bed, not surrounded by machines any more, but waving frantically at us in what was definitely a 'come in' kind of way.

'Hey!' she said, as we pushed the door open.

'Hi,' I said, feeling a bit awkward. 'Wow, you look loads better.' She really did. Her hair was back to shiny normal, her skin was clear and not nearly as pale any more and even though she was still really thin, she looked happy and more Angel-ish again.

'I *am* loads better, thanks to you three.' She grinned. 'It's really good to see you again.'

Almost every spare space in the room was filled

with cards, flowers and bunches of grapes. Some of the bouquets were humongous, and I suddenly felt a bit embarrassed at the tiny bunch we'd brought the previous Saturday. As I looked around, though, I saw they were on the little table right next to Angel's bed.

'Sit down,' said Angel. 'I've got loads to tell you.'

Er, hello – a megastar model with loads to tell *us*? Soph practically fainted with happiness on the spot. We each grabbed a chair. Angel was wearing these seriously cute spotty PJs and sitting cross-legged on top of the hospital blankets – a classic gossiping position.

After saying thank you about a million times, she filled us in on everything that had happened over the past few months – how terrible she'd been feeling and how it was so embarrassing when she kept fainting in front of the cameras. And then how she'd woken up here over the weekend, and found out what had really been going on.

'It's been kind of bonkers here ever since,' she said. 'All the newspaper articles – telling the truth this time – and people phoning to see when I'll be back at work. My agent from SuperModels has been in to see me every day and she's constantly texting when she's not here. They've been really worried, but I've got more bookings than ever since everything was sorted out,' she said. 'I'm doing magazines and catwalk shows and more stuff for Teen Shimmer.'

'So you're totally better, then?' I checked.

Angel wrinkled her nose. 'The doctors say I need to take at least three or four weeks off. They're letting me out of here at the weekend, though, and I'm going to use some of the money I've earned to take Mum, Dad and Frankie on holiday.'

'You must be totally relieved,' said Abs. 'You know, with Lysanne Rogers out of the way and everything getting back to normal.'

'It's horrible,' said Angel. 'Lysanne's been doing my make-up for ages and she always seemed really nice. We used to talk about all kinds of stuff. I thought we were friends. It's really freaky to think she was the person making me so ill.'

I traced a pattern on the floor with my toe, not sure what to say. When you thought about what could have happened to her, Angel was seriously lucky to be sitting here.

'Anyway,' she said, sounding more cheerful now, 'when I get back, the first modelling job I've got is at London Fashion Week. I'm doing this big catwalk show, and I wondered if you'd all like to come along and watch.'

'WOW!' squeaked Soph.

'I'll make sure they're front-row seats, so you get a good view,' she promised. 'I just really want you to be there.'

I thought Soph might explode.

'Isn't the front row where all the celebs sit?' asked Abs.

'Oui, oui! *Star Secrets* is always showing pics of them having a good goss about the clothes and the models and stuff,' I said. 'This is so amazing. Who d'you reckon we'll get to sit next to?'

'Girls Aloud?' Abs suggested.

'Maybe Mirage will be there,' said Soph.

'Or Maff.' Abs gave me a sneaky grin.

'What would Maff be doing at a fashion show?' I said.

As we talked, I noticed Angel check her watch and glance out of the window. It was actually about the third time she'd done it. Abs had obviously seen it, too. 'We'd better go,' she said, a bit awkwardly. 'You've probably got loads of important stuff to do.'

'NO!' said Angel. 'I mean, no – stay. It's really nice seeing all of you again. How's Whitney High?'

It seemed a bit of a weird question. If you were a jet-setting celeb living a life of total glitz and glamour, why on earth would you care about your stupid old school? And even if you did, why not just ask your sister about it instead of her friends?

'It's fine,' said Abs, looking as puzzled as I felt.

There was definitely something funny going on.

Angel fidgeted with her pillows. 'So, you never told me what actually happened,' she said. 'I mean, how you found out about Lysanne and what she was doing.'

'It was mostly thanks to my nan, actually,' I said. The chance to tell the story again made me forget the weirdness for a minute. 'She's into all of these detective shows on TV and we watched this très terrible film one night about two rival models.'

I carried on, telling Angel what had happened, with Abs and Soph chipping in as well. Just when we'd nearly finished, there was a knock at the door. Without waiting for an answer, a tall, thin woman in a black business suit walked into the room, carrying a silver briefcase.

'Angel, I'm so sorry,' she said, planting a kiss on each of Angel's cheeks. 'I know I said I'd be here sooner, but the traffic was awful.'

'It's fine,' said Angel. 'They're still here. Rosie, Abs, Soph – this is Emma Adams, Chief Executive of Teen Shimmer.'

Emma shook my hand so hard I thought my arm might drop off.

'Thrilled to meet you,' she said, moving on to shake hands with Abs and Soph, too. 'I was determined to thank you all in person.'

'It's really no problem,' I said, starting to feel a bit overwhelmed by all this gratitude.

'Not for you, maybe,' said Emma, 'but it was a dreadful time for everyone at Teen Shimmer. That's all behind us now, though.' She beamed. 'The new range is back on the shelves and selling like hot cakes. With all the bad publicity Glam Girls is getting, and everyone finding out we had nothing to do with Angel's illness, sales are higher than ever.'

'Can I tell them?' asked Angel.

Emma nodded.

'Tell us what?'

'They're going to name some of the stuff in the next range after the three of you,' said Angel.

'What?'

'No way!'

'You lie!'

'It's true,' said Emma. She opened her brief-case and handed us each a piece of paper with some sketches of make-up packaging and little name labels. 'Rosie Cheeks will be a new range of blushers, Soph*isticated is a perfume and Awesome Abs is body shimmer. They'll be in the shops by Christmas.'

Soph had to sit down then. It was all getting a bit much for her brain.

'Angel, I can't stay,' said Emma. Me, Abs and Soph were all being a bit goldfishy, still staring at the bits of paper. 'People to see, places to go. It was lovely meeting you, girls.'

'See you soon,' said Angel.

'Keep an eye on the postman,' said Emma, winking at us. Then she swept out of the room.

'Is she a bit nuts?' asked Abs.

'Yeah,' said Angel. 'Cool, isn't it?'

✳ ✳ ✳

A couple of days later, I was sitting in the kitchen staring miserably at my bowl of soggy breakfast cereal. Mum was upstairs thumping around, working out a new Banana Splits dance routine, and Nan was clinking spoons in the sink, already on her third cup of tea. It had been a pretty eventful week, but now things were back to normal and I had to admit I was feeling a bit gloomy. I knew we had Angel's fashion show and the new Teen Shimmer stuff to look forward to, but they seemed ages away. All I had to look forward to this weekend was a fat pile of French homework.

'Rosie, love, will you get that?' said Nan.

I looked up from my cereal, only just realising the doorbell had rung. I trudged along the hall and opened the front door.

'One for Miss Rosie Parker,' said the postie, handing me a massivo parcel, 'a few bills for Liz Parker and a letter for Mrs P. Parker.'

I took the envelopes and staggered back to the kitchen with the box.

'Gracious,' said Nan. 'What's in there?'

'No idea,' I shrugged, but as I said it, I remembered what Emma Adams had told us. *Keep an eye on the postman.* As quickly as I could, I tore the paper off and lifted the lid. Inside was what looked like one of every single item from the latest Teen Shimmer range – lipglosses, mascara, eye colours,

cheek tint, and in every colour you could imagine.
I picked up a note that was lying on top of the box.

Teen
Shimmer

Rosie

Here are a few goodies to say thanks
again. When you run out, ring the
number below and we'll send you some
more. I've added you to our VIP list, so
you'll get new products every time they
come out. See you at Fashion Week!

Emma Adams

A lifetime's supply of Teen Shimmer! I sank down
into my chair. Rosie Parker, speechless. Now there's
something that doesn't happen every day.

'Well, isn't that smashing?' said Nan.

'I know,' I said, peering into the box again. But
Nan wasn't looking at me. She was reading her
letter.

'Oh,' I said. 'Who's it from?'

'Fairy,' said Nan.

'Angel!' I corrected automatically, then realised what she'd said. 'Angel? What d'you mean?'

Nan handed me the letter.

Dear Mrs Parker

Thanks for all your help. Rosie says you're a fan of murder mysteries, so I thought you might like these. Have fun!

With love from Fairy
xxx

Clipped to the letter were two tickets for a murder-mystery weekend at one of those big fancy country mansions. I read the letter again and giggled. Frankie must have told Angel about Nan forgetting her name.

'Smashing,' said Nan again. 'I'll just put the kettle on for a nice cup of tea to celebrate. Now, where did I put those fig rolls?'

My life? Sometimes it's cool celebs and all the make-up I'll ever need; other times it's fig rolls and a family who make *The Simpsons* look normal.

It pretty much rocks.

Megastar

Everyone has blushing blunders - here are some from your Megastar Mystery friends!

Soph

I was walking round to Abs' house and my lips were feeling a bit dry so I nipped into the chemist and bought a raspberry-flavoured lip balm. After plastering some on, I bumped into Mr Adams. He was smiling at me so I smiled back and stopped for a chat. I got to Soph's place and she doubled over laughing. When I saw my reflection in the hallway mirror I wanted to die. My mouth was smeared messily in a dodgy shade of raspberry pink. It was a tinted lip balm! And I'd been talking to Mr Adams with a mouth like a clown! Oh, cringe, cringe, cringe!

Abs

I was on the bus with my little sister, Megan. I'd had some curry the night before and couldn't help letting out a silent-but-violent parp. I grabbed my perfume out my bag and pretended to be spraying it on, whilst cunningly covering up the smell. I thought I'd got away with it, when Megan suddenly yelled out, 'Yuck, Abs! Your perfume smells of windy-pops!' at the top of her voice. Everyone turned around and stared at me. I wanted the ground to swallow me up!

Cringes

Rosie

I'd been reading a feature in one of my mum's magazines about the importance of moisturising. There was a little sample stuck on the page next to it so I pulled it out and rubbed it on my face. The next morning, my entire face was all orangey-brown and streaky. I rushed to my bedroom found the sample in the bin. It wasn't moisturiser. It was fake tan for a 'long-lasting, deep holiday glow'. Mum wouldn't let me stay off school so I had to face the world with a face like a tangerine!

Angel

When I first went to America to model, I was invited to a celebrity fancy dress party. I'd just won the contract to be face of Teen Shimmer and it seemed like a really good idea to go dressed as make-up. I made a sparkly mascara outfit from foil-covered cardboard, but the costume was so tight around my legs I could hardly walk. I was sure I'd be fine after a bit of practise but I was sooo wrong. When I arrived at the party, I tripped over on the drive, and rolled down the slope. I couldn't get up again so I had to just lie there until somebody came to help me. Oh, the shame!

Ten Things NOT to Say to Time Lord

1. Oooh, tell us more about the time you were in *Doctor Who!*

2. Can we have some extra homework, please, Mr Lord?

3. If the Cybermen and the Daleks had a fight, who would win?

4. Who's the better Dr Who – Christopher Eccleston or David Tennant?

5. Can we do our vocal exercises in the style of a Darlek today?

6. Please, please make a guest appearance in our school play.

7. Did you know there's a famous person in town?

8. Can I try on your Cyberman helmet?

9. Hey, Mr Lord, lovin' your tie!

10. So, what kind of acting skills do you need to be an extra in *Doctor Who*?

Fact File

NAME: Pam Parker

AGE: 61

STAR SIGN: Capricorn

HAIR: Grey and permed

EYES: Hazel

LOVES: All things murder mystery

HATES: Liz and Rosie talking over her favourite TV programmes

LAST SEEN: In Trotters with a cup of tea, an iced bun and detective novel

MOST LIKELY TO SAY: 'What would Jessica Fletcher do?'

WORST CRINGE EVER: Coming out of the ladies loo at a service station in Fleetwich to discover she had the back of her raincoat tucked into her tights. It'd never happen to Miss Marple!

Angel Face

Crystal clear

Make a gentle cleanser by soaking a few slices of cucumber in water for half an hour. Then dip a cotton wool pad in the liquid and gently sweep it across your face. Once you've finished, rinse your face with warm water and pat it dry with a fluffy towel.

Fresh-faced

Want to mix up a relaxing facemask? All you need is one tablespoonful of porridge oats and two tablespoons of natural yoghurt. Spread the mixture on your face, taking care to avoid the area around your eyes. Lean back and relax for five minutes, then use a clean flannel to wipe away the mask and rinse your face with warm water.

Eau, yes!

OK, I know everyone goes on about it, but water really is good for your looks. It flushes out your system and keeps everything working nicely. So, if you want bright eyes and healthy skin, aim to drink a couple of litres a day. If I get bored with drinking plain water, I add a dash of orange juice to make it more interesting. Give it a go!

Get a model look with Angel's expert beauty tips

Pearly smile

If you want to make an impression, you need a Hollywood smile! Keep your teeth pearly white by steering clear of sugary snacks and brushing regularly. Try using a special plaque-busting mouthwash as well and your teeth will soon be bright enough to light up Hollywood Boulevard!

Good hair days

If your hair has a mind of its own, just work out a few rescue hairdos that are quick and easy. Accessorise your locks with sparkly hairclips for a hint of glamour, or if you want a surfy look, go for low bunches or pretty plaits.

Happy feet

Make a revitalising foot soak with a few sprigs of natural mint in a bowl of warm water. Put the bowl on a towel to stop any spills, pop your feet in the water and sit back for five minutes. There's no need to rinse your feet when you've finished, just pat them dry with a towel.

Strike a Pose

Find out what kind of model you'd be with this cool quiz

Q3:
'The way I look is more important than my personality.' How true of you is this statement?
a. So true
b. Totally false

Q1:
If you were a model, what do you think would be the most important, getting the best dressing room or getting the best outfit?
a. Dressing room
b. Outfit

Q4:
Are you always the first one in front of the camera?
a. Yes! Show me the flash bulbs, baby!
b. Not so much. I prefer taking the photos

Q2:
Which of the following do you prefer?
a. Spending hours at the hairdressers
b. Going shopping with your friends

Q5:

You turn up at a party wearing the same dress as your friend. Do you? . . .

a. Run screaming from the building
b. Make a big joke about the whole thing

Cover Girl

You hate anyone stealing your limelight, and you always have to look your best. Honey, you are sooo a cover girl in training! You've got the patience of a supermodel, too, which will come in handy for all those long days in the studio.

Most likely to say: 'Can we re-shoot please, and this time could you only take pictures of my best side?'

Catwalk Cool

You've got bags of personality and you love being in front of a crowd. You'd make a great catwalk model because you're always ready to listen to what people want. If you were a model, designers would be beating a path to your door!

Most likely to say: 'So, you're going for space-city alien kind of vibe with this dress? I can do that!'

Q6:

Where would you rather go on holiday?

a. Anywhere near a shopping mall will do just fine
b. Somewhere with lots of trees to hide behind

Camera Shy

OK, so you may think you've got no chance at all, but that's really not true. Plenty of top models have shy moments. It's all part of the job. Practise posing in front of the camera and you'll soon be on your way to model stardom!

Most likely to say: 'Wouldn't you rather take some nice pictures of the countryside?'

Soph's Style Tips

FUNKY, FRINGED T-SHIRT

Turn an old T-shirt into a going-out
top. Cut 10-centimetre strips vertically
from the bottom of your T-shirt to make
an even fringe. Thread some beads
on each fringe and tie it in a knot. Voilà!

GET GLOWING

Get some glow-in-the-dark fabric paint
and draw some stars on an old pair of
jeans. You'll look totally cool when the
lights go down!

BRILLIANT BEADS!

For a très original piece of jewellery,
buy a few old necklaces from a charity
shop and use the different beads to make
a totally new necklace.

Are you ready to hear the coolest style tips around?

LUSH LAYERS

If you want to look completely *Vogue*, go for the layered look. Just wear a few colour-coordinating tops over each other and team them with a gillet. Don't forget to layer your accessories, too. Grab a bunch of bracelets and bangles and try wearing a few necklaces at the same time.

BLACK IS THE NEW BLACK

Black is a totally stylish colour and it goes with everything. Try wearing a black top with a black necklace. Or a chic pair of black skinny jeans with a tight T-shirt. Très Parisian!

Rosie's Guide to Palm Reading

Heart Line

Head Line

Life Line

The Life Line

The life line starts between the thumb and the index finger. If it's strong, it means that you're full of energy, and if it's faint, it probably means that you haven't handed in your maths homework.

The Head Line

The head line runs horizontally from the middle of the palm to the heart line. It's all about memory, intelligence and reasoning. Celebrity sleuths have very strong head lines!

The Heart line

The heart line runs horizontally across the upper palm. A long line means that you are a loving and giving kind of girl. But if it's short, you're probably Amanda Hawkins.

Liz Parker's Guide to

BANANARAMA

(with comments by Rosie Parker)

Bananarama are the best girl band in the history of music

Er, on whose planet, Mum?

They were formed in 1981

1981, 1891 . . . like, what's the difference?

The band members are Siobhan Fahey, Sara Dallin and Keren Woodward

Shhh – you're taking up valuable space in my brain. If I fail my GCSEs, I think we'll know who's fault it is, that's all I'm saying.

Bananarama's top hits include:

T'ain't What You Do (It's the Way That You Do It)

Not the way you do it, Mum . . .

Really Saying Something

Well, that's a matter of opinion . . .

Na Na Hey Hey Kiss Him Goodbye

Like, are they a girl band or the Teletubbies?

Cruel Summer

Sure was if Bananarama had a hit in the charts

Robert De Niro's Waiting

For you to stop singing, perhaps?

Love in the First Degree

Mum?! How could you even mention this song? Since you recorded me singing it and sent the DVD in for the whole school to see, people have been humming the chorus each time I walk into a room. Ha, ha. Not.

How Nosy Are You?

- ♥ Mystery books are sooo dull
- 🔒 I think of myself as a young Miss Marple (a very, very young Miss Marple, in fact!)
- ♥ Celeb gossip is totally boring
- ★ I like to know what's going on in everyone's lives
- 🔒 My favourite word is 'why?'
- ♥ My mates are the most important people, ever!
- ★ I am obsessed with celebrity mags!
- 🔒 I would rummage through people's bins if I thought they were up to something!
- ★ I love mystery programmes on TV

See if you're even nosier than Rosie Parker!
Choose the five sentences that sound most
like you, see how many of each symbol you got
and read your answer!

★ I hate to feel like I'm missing out on anything

♥ I'm happiest just being in my room

🔒 I'm always checking what the neighbours are up to!

Mostly heart symbols: Gossip-free Gwen

Hmmm, you have absolutely no interest in gossip at all! You're happy just knowing what's going on with you and your mates and couldn't care less if a celeb has just bought a dress that cost most than your house! Not being nosy makes your life pretty chilled, but is it fun?!

Mostly star symbols: Curious Cat

You're fairly nosy and like to know all the latest celeb news, but you'd never go as far as looking in a bin or sneaking into someone's house! You save your nosiness for celebs and people you don't really know, that way you can't get into too much trouble!

Mostly lock symbols: Nosy Rosie

Wow, you're almost as nosy as Rosie! You love knowing who's up to what and wouldn't think twice about doing what Rosie does. Just make sure you don't get into trouble! Being nosy can be fun, but not if it means you end up behind bars!

Pam's Problem Page

Never fear, Pam's here to sort you out!

Dear Pam,

I've got a terrible outbreak of spots and I can't help thinking that somebody might be trying to sabotage my modelling career by poisoning me. How can I tell?

Angel

Pam says: Spots are not a symptom of poisoning, so don't you worry yourself. I once saw an episode of Murder, She Wrote, where Jessica's favourite nephew was being poisoned. He had an agonising stomach ache, but no spots, so I think you can rest assured. If you were being poisoned, you'd probably be really ill, and I'm sure a bright girl like you would notice if your orange juice tasted a bit funny. Lots of young girls get spots, dearie. It's all part of growing up. Just accept them and get on with your life.

Can't wait for the next
book in the series?
Here's a sneak preview of

Honeydale

Chapter One

I still couldn't believe it. Me, Rosie Parker, on my way to London to be a journalist – a JOURNALIST! – on *Star Secrets* magazine. It was only the best mag in the country, if not the universe. Basically, it was the bestissimo thing since cheesy chips, with brilliant features, quizzes, fashion and, most importantly, the most fantasticissimo celebrity interviews. And I was going to work on it. I mean, that could be it – my big break. I could become the best celebrity writer they'd ever had. I could end up a totally famous writer with loads of cool celebrity friends, who'd all give speeches about how they'd never have made it without me. And a film company would make a movie of my life and huge stars like Hilary Duff and Lindsay Lohan would fight over who got to play me. OK, so neither Hilary nor Lindsay had birds' nests masquerading for hair, or one annoying bit of eyebrow which permanently stuck out at a très attractive 90-degree angle from their head, no matter what they try, but hey, it was my movie. Oooh, I could just see the gossip columns:

LATEST GOSSIP JUST IN!

Which famous film star had a near miss when another A-lister poured champagne over her at a star-studded celebrity party? The attacker refused to apologise. 'She deserved it,' she told shocked fellow diners. 'She's landed the part of Rosie Parker. It's only the biggest role in film history!' Upon hearing this, five other female stars had to be restrained from bashing the victim over the head with their It-bags.

My mobile beeped, snapping me back to the present. Oooh, text message from Abs:

> **Still can't believe me and Soph R stuck in Bore-ing-hurst while U have wk's work experience on Star Secrets. We'll miss U!! X :-(**

OK, OK, so maybe I was getting a little carried away. It wasn't like this was a permanent job. But then I'm only 14 – there are laws against children working full-time, y'know. Work-experience slots on *Star Secrets* are like gold dust – seriously, they're rarer than Simon Cowell's compliments. It says in the front of the magazine that there aren't any available for the next two years, so there's no point ringing up trying to get one. So how did I manage to swing it? Well, basically *Star Secrets* ran a competition to write a story and the prize was not only to have the winning story published in – yep, you guessed it – *Star Secrets*, but also a week's work experience. I couldn't believe it when I got the phone call to say I'd won. Literally couldn't believe it. In fact, I made a bit of an idiot of myself. The conversation went something like this:

Me: *Hello.*

Woman's voice: *Hi. Could I speak to Rosie Parker, please?*

Me: *Speaking.*

Woman's voice: *Hi, Rosie. This is Belle Clarkson, editor of* Star Secrets.

Me: *Yeah, right.*

Woman's voice: *Er, sorry?*

Me: *If you're Belle Clarkson, I'm the sixth member of Girls Aloud.*

Woman's voice: *Rosie, I can assure you, I am Belle Clarkson.*

Me: *Look, I know it's you, Amanda Hawkins. If it isn't enough that you already made an idiot of me at school today by pointing out to the whole class that I had a massivo streamer of toilet roll attached to my shoe, now you're trying to torment me in the evenings, too. Well,* *it's about time you got yourself a life. Why don't you just go back to Loserville with all your loser friends and get lost?*

Woman's voice: *Um, right. Rosie? Look, I'm really not Amanda, um, Dorkins, was it?*

Me: *[starting to giggle] Dorkins? Dorkins? As in dork? That's hilarious! I think another school nickname might just have been born. But hang on a minute – if you're not Amanda Dork-Hawkins, that means you really are . . .*

Woman's voice: *Belle Clarkson, Editor of* Star Secrets.

OOPS!

Fortunately, Belle saw the funny side. In fact, she said I'd made her day, although she might have changed her mind after I screamed at the top of my lungs when she told me I'd won the competition. Not only would my story be published in one of the April issues of *Star Secrets*, but my work experience was fixed for school half-term!

So that's why I was now pulling my suitcase off

the luggage shelf as the train pulled into London Waterloo, accidentally hitting the woman in front of me on the head in my rush. To say that I was totally excited would be a bit of an understatement.

Penny was waiting for me by the ticket barrier, looking totally amazing in skinny jeans, black knee-high boots and a battered grey leather jacket. Penny is my best friend Soph's aunt, and basically the coolest person *ever*, and I was staying at her flat for the week. She's a fashion stylist and totally knows EVERYONE worth knowing – including loads of celebs. Penny gets to hang out with famous people all the time. But, like the professional she is, she never gets star-struck. Which, when you think about it, is probably a very good thing. I mean, just imagine if you were styling a huge star, like Madonna, and you got a fit of nerves just as you were doing up her dress, and you ended up breaking the zip and having to cut her out? Talk about embarrassing! Anyway, Penny says most celebs are just ordinary, decent people who happen to have amazing lives.

As soon as she spotted me, she ran forward and gave me a massive hug. 'Rosie! You look fab. How are you?'

Without waiting for an answer, she ushered me out of the station and towards the main road, talking nineteen to the dozen.

'It's so great to have you here again,' she said, stepping into the road and expertly flagging down a passing taxi, much to the annoyance of everyone who was patiently queuing in the taxi rank on the other side of the street. You could so tell who Soph took after in her family. Ignoring the disgruntled shouts of 'Oi, there's a queue here,' and 'Who does she think she is?' Penny hustled me into the taxi and, giving the driver her address, leant back into the seat to give me her full attention.

'I can't wait to hear all your news. And I can't believe you won a week's work experience on *Star Secrets*. That's totally amazing!' she said. 'I bet Soph and Abs are greener than a frog with travel sickness! It's such a shame you couldn't all come; it would have been great fun.'

The original plan had been for me, Abs and Soph to stay all week. We'd all stayed once before when Penny had swung us jobs as runners on the film set where Paige and Shelby Sweetland, the famous Australian celebrity twins, were making their latest movie. But Soph had been given extra shifts at Dream Beauty, the salon where she had a Saturday job, which meant she couldn't make it. Then Abs's Aunt Stacey (she's nowhere *near* as cool as Penny – well, not unless sensible shoes, kilts and hand-knitted jumpers have suddenly become the height of fashion) rang and said she was visiting from Canada. Of course, Abs's parents wouldn't hear of her not being there to see her, so that left little old me.

'I hope you don't mind, but my friend Sally is coming round for dinner tonight. I couldn't cancel. She's a make-up artist on that soap *Honeydale,* which means she's been working flat out and I haven't seen her for ages.'

'*Honeydale?*' I sat bolt upright, staring at Penny in amazement. 'Are you *serious?*'

'Yup,' Penny nodded, grinning at me as soon as

she saw the look on my face.

'I LOVE *Honeydale* – it's my favourite soap. I never miss an episode! I can't *believe* you know someone who works on it.'

'So I'm guessing you don't mind that Sally's coming over for dinner, then?' Penny said, smiling and rifling around in her bag for her purse as the taxi pulled up outside her building. I was practically skipping with excitement as I clambered out. Could this week get any better?

As Penny unlocked the front door, her mobile started ringing. 'Make yourself at home,' she said, flicking open her phone. 'I won't be a mo.'

I love Penny's flat. It's exactly the kind of place I dream of living in when I'm older, earning loads of money as a mega-successful writer. Everything's cream, which may sound boring, but Penny's added funky cushions, curtains and the most amazing paintings to give it splashes of colour. But the bestissimo thing about Penny's flat is her walk-in wardrobe. As a stylist, Penny's always being given loads of free stuff – cast-offs donated from the celebrities she styles, freebies from designers who are desperate for her to dress celebs in their stuff . . . Basically, she gets sent so many free products and so much make-up she could start her own shop. I'm not joking. The amount of stuff in her wardrobe is dizzying. I mean, literally.

Soph said the first time she saw the flat, just after Penny had moved in, she opened the wardrobe door to reveal shelf after shelf of neatly stacked tops and jumpers, and rows of skirts, trousers, coats, shoes and boots. After staring for a long time, Soph said, 'I think I might faint.' I'm not kidding. She had to sit down on the floor with her head between her knees and breathe deeply for about five minutes. See? Seriously dizzy-making.

I flopped down on one of the two huge, squishy sofas in the lounge. A few minutes later, Penny wandered in, looking annoyed.

'That was Sally on the phone. She's not coming tonight. She's still at the studio and says she's going to have to work late.' She plonked herself down on to the sofa next to me. 'This is the fourth time she's let me down now. I'm torn between feeling completely irritated and worrying about her. We always used to meet up at least once a week for a good old gossip, but since she's started on *Honeydale* I've hardly seen her – she's lost loads of weight and is totally stressed.'

'Oh, no!' I said. 'That's a shame.' I meant it, too – I had been looking forward to hearing all the gossip about *Honeydale*. I bet Sally knew all the latest soap stories and I couldn't wait to hear what all the stars were really like. Especially Cassie St Clair, who was, like, the biggest soap star ever in soap history. Seriously, I bet even the Pope had heard of her!

Penny smiled at me, 'Not to worry. It means we can have a nice evening together, plus you should get an early night – after all, it's your first day at *Star Secrets* tomorrow, don't forget!'

Yeah, right. As if I was ever going to forget that!

ENDEAVOUR BOOKS